Princeton University

The Decennial Record of the Class of 1881 of Princeton College

Princeton University

The Decennial Record of the Class of 1881 of Princeton College

ISBN/EAN: 9783337169626

Printed in Europe, USA, Canada, Australia, Japan

Cover: Foto ©Andreas Hilbeck / pixelio.de

More available books at **www.hansebooks.com**

THE

DECENNIAL RECORD

OF

THE CLASS OF 1881

OF

PRINCETON COLLEGE

PRESS OF

JOHN H. WILLIAMS & CO.

BALTIMORE, MD.

In compiling this Record of the various fortunes of the members of the Class during the past ten years your Committee has endeavored to preserve the individuality of each report as far as possible by giving it in its original form. We regret that the excessive modesty of certain members has supplied us with such meagre records and that we have not been able to live up to our ambition of giving at least the address and some brief account of every living member of the Class. We have labored diligently towards this end because we believe that every man in the Class feels *some* interest in the career of every other man, even though the feeling be nothing more than curiosity to learn whether in ten years he has turned out better or worse than an association with him of four years or less gave reason to expect. Does the history of the first ten years spent in "the wide, wide world" by the Class of 1881, Princeton College, tend to show that a college education pays? In ten years more this question will begin to acquire a practical importance for those who were our foremost competitors for the Class Cup.

But whatever the fortunes of her children there can be no doubt as to the prosperity of our Alma Mater, and the record of the changes during the past ten years cannot fail to be noted with pride by every loyal son of Princeton.

The description of the Class Memorial by Prof. Marquand together with the report of the Memorial Committee and the pictures of the casts, which by the courtesy of the Committee we are able to present, all unite to assure us of a just pride in our Memorial and its substantial value to the College. An account of the Decennial Reunion will be of interest to all who were unable to be present.

But the changes of the years have brought with them loss as well as gain, sorrow as well as rejoicing, and we mourn the death of nine classmates who graduated with us ten years ago. The death of our President, beyond question our most representative man, fell like a blow on every member of the Class and the brilliant promise of the career of Bruce made his early death a peculiar loss.

In concluding these introductory remarks the Committee desires to express again to the Memorial Committee appreciation of its kindness in having prepared the pictures of the various pieces and groups of the Memorial Collection, and to Prof. Marquand thanks for the interesting description of the Collection he has so kindly prepared for the benefit of the Class. The Committee also desires to acknowledge the kindness of Messrs. Blydenburgh and Munn in furnishing much valuable information contained in the sketch of the College during the past ten

iv

years, and to thank several members of the Class for having honored so generously the drafts made upon their time in hunting up the lost and strayed, stirring up the dilatory and obtaining information about the dumb. As the work of gathering materials for the Record went on your Committee has grown more and more grateful to those who sent news of themselves and sent that news promptly.

J. LEVERETT MOORE

THOMAS D. WARREN

ARTHUR L. KIMBALL, Chairman,

Committee on Decennial Record.

ILLUSTRATIONS

vi

CONTENTS

ALLEN, F. P. "In the fall of '81 I accepted the position of Chief Engineer of a contracting company, but the spring following, my health being poor, I gave up the place and after a few weeks rest started for Dakota to recuperate. On the way I picked up "Dad" Walsh, who was then living in St. Paul, and we journied together to Miles City, Mont., at that time the end of the N. P. R. R.

I will not attempt to describe our ludicrous adventures, for Walsh might object as he has now settled down in life and become the dignified and happy father of a young son and heir. [How about yourself, Frank?] Suffice it to say that we returned safely to civilization and I stopped at Jamestown, Dak., while "Hob" returned to his home in St. Paul. Soon after I came down to Lisbon and started the Ransom County Bank, but sold it out during the following winter and engaged in the Real Estate and Loan business. Since leaving College I had spent all my spare time in studying law, and about this time I was admitted to practice in the District, and subsequently in the Supreme Court.

I was married Sept. 1, 1886, to Miss Minnie L. Taft at her home in Ballston Spa., N. Y. and on Aug. 3, '87, a little daughter was born to us.

In the fall of 1886 I was elected County Judge of Ransom County, but after serving out my term declined a renomination and formed a partnership for the practice of law under the firm name of Rouke & Allen. Since settling in Lisbon I have filled the offices of City Clerk, Alderman, County Justice of the Peace, Commissioner of Insanity, County Judge and County Surveyor."

ARCHER, J. R. No report. We have understood that he is still engaged in mining in Virginia.

ARMSTRONG, A. C., JR. "1881-2 Fellow of Princeton College, 1882-5 student in Princeton Theological Seminary, 1885-6 studied at the University of Berlin, 1886-7 Associate Professor of Ecclesiastical History in Princeton Theological Seminary, 1887-8 Assistant Editor of the *New Princeton Review*, and Instructor in History, Princeton College, from 1888 Professor of Philosophy in Wesleyan University.

Married in Princeton, Sept. 6, 1888, Miss Mabel Chester Murray, daughter of Rev. Dr. James O. Murray, Professor of English Literature in Princeton College and Dean of the Faculty. A son, Andrew Campbell Armstrong, 3rd, was born June 5th, 1890; and died at Princeton April 10th, 1891.

In June, 1889, was elected member of Phi Beta Kappa Fraternity, Wesleyan Chapter. I have published a number of articles in reviews and newspapers, but they have been mostly forgotten and none are of permanent value."

BACOT, W. S. After graduation turned his attention wholly to Civil Engineering, preparatory to which he had already had some special training in the School of Science, as a special student under Prof. McMillan, and agreeably to his advice made a special study of Hydraulic

Engineering. Has since been engaged in the practice of this branch in connection with other work from 1881 down to the present time, acting as Assistant and Chief Engineer in the construction of various water-works, tunnels, etc. Was appointed Chief Engineer of County Roads, Richmond Co., N. Y. on July 8th, 1890, and still holds the position. Is also Engineer of Roads in the village of Lenox, Mass., and Asst. Engineer City of Albany New Water supply.

Is a member of the American Society of Civil Engineers, devoted to his profession, and doing well in it. Still remains single.

BARRET, C. R. No report. Opened a private banking house in Louisville, Ky., about four years ago, which failed last Fall. Went abroad and when last heard of was in India. Is still unmarried.

BEDELL, F. L. "On graduating from College I took up the study of the law, but after an argument with Blackstone of more than two years duration, I became convinced that there was little room, especially at the top, for any more legal lights to shine in this community. I therefore blew mine out and accepted the position of private secretary to the junior partner in an importing house in New York City. Here I remained until January 1885, when I resigned to accept a position with the Prudential Insurance Company, in which I became Asst. Actuary, and afterwards manager of the Claim Department, the position I still hold.

In January, 1886, I was married to Miss Matilda Webb, of Newark. We lost an infant daughter, and have one child living, a boy of four, who is a loyal friend of

3

Princeton, and already has gone into active training for the Foot-ball Team of 1905."

BLYDENBURGH, B. B. "On leaving College I entered the Columbia College Law School and graduated there in 1883. The following year I was admitted to the New York bar, and have since practiced in New York, having my office at 111 Broadway. I am unmarried."

BRADFORD, T. B., is a physician. Graduated from Univ. of Penn. in '84. Spent a year and a half as resident in the Episcopal Hospital of Philadelphia, with a year's special course in Surgery and Gynæcology in Univ. of Penn. Hospital. Is now Surgeon to the Delaware Hospital. Was married Dec. 18th, 1888, at Wilmington, Del., to Miss Helen Rogers. One child, Thomas Budd, Jr., born Feb. 4th, 1890.

. BRANT, H. L. Graduated at Columbia College Law School in 1884. After serving a clerkship of four years in New York, opened an office, and began the practice of the law, which is his present occupation. Married to Miss Nellie L. Chase, at Newark, N. J., Nov. 26th, 1885, Two children, Clifford Augustus, born Dec. 11th, 1887, Hazel Chase, June 23rd, 1890. Has not been called upon to fill any "position of honor or trust", aside from that of Pater Familias, and offices in various religious and beneficial organizations.

BRECKINRIDGE, D. C. "After graduating studied Law and practiced the same for 4½ years with my Father in St. Louis. Two years ago came to New York, entered the partnership of Martin & Breckinridge, and on the death of my partner having succeeded to the business, am now carrying it on myself under the partnership name.

4

My business deals with Railway Supplies and Equipment, Railroad Securities, and the construction of Railways, both Steam and Street, Horse and Electric.

Am still unfortunately single, though having tried in vain to be otherwise—a sad commentary on the taste of the gentler sex. Have never filled any position of honor, never been guilty of writing a book, and have done nothing to make my Class proud of me, except to eat a very good dinner at the last Alumni Banquet here.''

BROWN, S. "My *profession* is law (I am glad you did not ask for a *confession*), and I am Master in Chancery of United States Circuit Court for Southern District of Illinois.

I was married April 28th, 1886, to Miss Kate Logan Hay, and have one child, a boy, Milton Hay, born April 2nd, 1887.''

ADAM TODD BRUCE died of fever at Ismailia, Egypt, Feb. 9th, 1887, in the twenty-eighth year of his age.

The year after graduation he took a position in the Laurenceville School, and part of his instruction being in Natural History, his attention was turned to Biology. He was a member of the Western Expedition of '82, and in the fall returned to Princeton as Demonstrator in Comparative Anatomy. The next year he was elected a Fellow of the Johns Hopkins University, and Fellow by Courtesy in 1885. He took his degree as Doctor of Philosophy in June 1886, and during the following summer was appointed Instructor in Osteology and Mammalian Anatomy in the University. He entered on his work with great energy and enthusiasm, but this fresh responsibility, added to the labors of original research, overtaxed his strength, and towards the close of November he was obliged to give up all work for a time, and started with his family on an extended tour in search of rest and recuperation. After remaining for some time in London he decided upon a voyage to Egypt through the Straits and made the trip by himself, joining his family, who had come by land, at Alexandria, whence they all went to Cairo and Ismailia. At the latter place he was attacked by fever—and the end came.

The following is a brief account of a largely attended meeting of Bruce's friends and pupils in the Biological Lecture Room of the Johns Hopkins University. Prof. Martin took the Chair, and among other remarks said : "Surely no death is so sad as that of a young man, who has just completed seven or eight years of hard work at college and university, and is beginning to enjoy the fruits of his labors. Such was the death which is the occasion of this meeting.

Dr. Bruce's researches as published* are known to most of you. They are all morphological and for the most part connected with arthropod embryology; although last Summer, while at Wood's Holl, he performed and published important work in regard to the development of the Squid. As regards his work on the early embryology of Insects, Dr. Brooks told me that Bruce had discovered more than all previous workers on the subject put together. During the earlier months of this session he was engaged in preparing in common with Dr. Brooks a monograph on the development of the King Crab.

Though devoted to morphological work Bruce was not narrow in his sympathies or pursuits. He had a great fondness for English literature, especially the older litera-

---

* For list of published articles, see *J. H. U. Circulars* No. 54.

ture, and had a very extensive knowledge of it. At Princeton his studies were largely philosophical while he was an undergraduate, and after coming here he did considerable psychological work under the direction of Prof. Stanley Hall. His handsome vigorous frame, his bright pleasant face, his manly honest look made all who met him inclined at once to like him; and those who knew him esteemed him more the more they knew him. So that between those who loved him for himself, and those who esteemed him for his work and those who were his comrades in athletics, he had among us a very large number of friends, representing many departments and many interest in the University."

Dr. Kimball, who had been a classmate of Dr. Bruce at Princeton, then said a few words in regard to the esteem in which Dr. Bruce had there been held, and proposed the adoption of the following preamble and resolutions:

Whereas, We have learned with profound sorrow of the death of Dr. Adam T. Bruce, the friend of all and the instructor of many of us,—and

Whereas, He had while here especially endeared himself to us by his unfailing kindness and courtesy,—be it

Resolved, That, assembled here today, in love of the memory of the pleasant companionship which existed between him and us in all relations, official and personal, we hereby express our grief that he was not spared to return among us,—and

Resolved, That we tender to his immediate friends and family our sincere sympathy in their bereavement,—and

Resolved, That a copy of these resolutions be forwarded to the Editor of the University Circulars, to the

7

Faculty of Princeton College, and to the family of Dr. Bruce.

The following gentlemen also spoke of the high regard and affection with which they remembered Dr. Bruce, viz.: Mr. Riggs, Prof. Hall, Mr. Burton and Pres. Gilman *

It was suggested in a letter by Dr. Brooks, who at the time was in Nassau, that the publication of Bruce's thesis on "The Germ-Layers of Insects and Arachnids" would be the best testimonial to the value of his investigations. Accordingly through the kindness of friends in the University, Princeton and elsewhere, the volume appeared in February 1888, with an introduction by Dr. Brooks.

In May 1887 the Trustees of the University accepted from the hands of Bruce's mother the sum of $10,000 to be used in founding as a memorial "The Adam T. Bruce Fellowship in Biology".

Butler, C. H. "I am an attorney and counsellor at law practicing in the City of New York, and member of the firm of Holt & Butler, organized in 1884. I was married at Yonkers, N. Y., November 21st, 1882 to Miss Marcia Flagg and have three children, all living, viz., Ethan Flagg, born January 4, 1884, Marcia Flagg, born July 4, 1886, Charles Marshall, born December 28, 1887.

Beyond having served for two years as Alderman for the Third Ward of the City of Yonkers, I have not filled any political position. I have not written a book, made any important discovery or done anything to my knowledge requiring the Class to erect a monument to my memory."

---

* Taken from *Johns Hopkins University Circulars*, No. 57, April, 1887.

S

CAULDWELL, T. W. "Since leaving College I have given my time to the study and practice of the law in New York State. On Oct. 21, 1884, I was married in New York to Miss Caroline S. Johnson, of that City. We have one child, Elizabeth M., born Jan. 22, 1888."

CORY, L. No report. Is a member of firm of Church & Cory, lawyers, Fresno, California. Married Oct. 17, 1882, to Miss Carrie A. Martin. Three children. Edith Marie, born March 10, 1884, Catherine, born August 17, 1887, and Esther, born March 29, 1891.

COWSEN, W. A. JR.
2. Lawyer—practicing in Graham, Young Co. Texas.
3. Single.
4. Was in office of Corporation Counsel of New York City for about three years.

COWAN, J. F. "I came to Butte, Montana, September 1881 and engaged in the livery business for four years. I then bought some placer mining ground and water rights near Butte, and have since engaged in mining, and supplying the mills and smelters with coal and wood. The water rights became quite valuable and were sold last fall at a good advance. I am a member of the City Council and have managed to escape the penitentiary thus far. I have become a greater "gun-crank" even than when I was in College and won the Championship Cup of Montana last August in Helena, scoring 92 birds out of 100.

I was married July 10, 1883 to Miss Stella Joslin in Oregon, Mo., and have three children, one boy and two girls. They can all give "the tiger" and the boy practices drop-kicks with his sisters' hat and keeps everybody in

9

the house dodging his "out-curves". So you see I am training him to be a true Princetonian."

COYLE, J. L. "My business is insurance. Was formerly for several years a pedagogue. Am a widower at present, but intend to marry again in a few months. I was married in 1885, and my wife died in 1886. I have one daughter. My wife's maiden name was Clara B. Vanderhoof. Child's name Clara, born Sept. 30, 1886.

Am a Committee on R. Rs., and call on all friends to force R. Rs. to give decent accommodations and run trains on time."

CRAVEN, C. E. "For two years after leaving College I taught in the York Collegiate Institute, York, Pa., and then entered the Seminary at Princeton in the Class of '86. I was ordained June 15, '86 pastor of the Presbyterian Church of Birmingham, Pa., were I remained until the fall of '88, when I came to my present charge, the Central Presbyterian Church, Downingtown, Pa.

I was married in York, Pa., Dec. 28, 1886 to Miss Anna Schenck McDougall and have two little daughters, Virginia Coryell, born Nov. 8th, '87, and Sarah Laudreth, born Oct. 18th, '89."

Charlie was one of the Lynde Debate judges this year.—Eds.

EDWARD F. CROSBY died at Helena, Montana, May 16, 1890 in the thirty-second year of his age.

Crosby studied law in Newport, R. I., and was admitted to the Bar there and afterwards in New York. He went to Helena, Mont., and entered the employ of the First National Bank. He also continued to practice law and undertook some journalistic work, as correspondent for some of the newspapers there and in New York ; a series of his letters from Alaska were extensively copied throughout the country. Later he went into Real Estate operations. He enjoyed the confidence of the community in which he lived and died leaving many friends.

He married in Helena the daughter of the Right Rev. Leigh R. Brewer, Episcopal Bishop of Montana, and his wife and child, a little girl, survive him.

DANFORTH, C. "My business is that of a raw silk importer, with the firm of Wm. Ryle & Co. Was married April 8, 1886, at Paterson, N. J., to Claudia E. Greppo. Have two children, Charles Ryle, born Jan. 21, 1887, and Claudia, born July 18, 1888."

DARDEN, W. H. "My profession has been the Gospel Ministry. After completing my studies at the San Francisco Theological Seminary I took charge of three churches near here,—a Presbyterian Home Missionary circuit. Three years later, the field opened up here at Petaluma, and we organized a church, to which I was called; and here, in spite of the changes so common on this coast among our churches, I have remained. We have received 150 members into this church, and still we number only 80. This will give you some idea of the constant changes that are going on in this Western world.

I was married April 16, 1884, to Miss Fanny D. Barlow. We have two children, Rena Elizabeth, born Jan. 7, 1888, and William Earl, born March 14, 1890. Nothing would give me greater pleasure than to attend the Decennial Reunion."

DAVIS, F. M. "My history since leaving Princeton has been uneventful. I did not study a profession, but immediately after graduation went into the machinery business in Liberty St. N. Y. City. There I remained for 5½ years, where I entered the house of H. G. Craig & Co., Commission Merchants, 132 Nassau St., N. Y., with whom I still continue, for it would be extremely difficult to find a more agreeable position.

Entered into the married condition Feb. 7, 1884 with Miss Augusta M. Stalker, and am the proud father of two fine boys, Raymond Foster, born April 25, 1885 and Charles Moreau Jr., born April 7, 1888. They are both bound for Princeton and will reach it I hope in due time.

Have not written a book, nor made a discovery, except that the married state is far better than the single. Have occupied several positions in the church, in societies, etc., and even dabbled a little in politics, but have gained no reputation outside of the town in which I reside and not very much in it.''

Davis, W. C. "I left Princeton College in June, 1879. In the fall of that year I entered the law office of Hon. Andrew Reed, at Lewistown, Pa., as a student, and was admitted to practice in the courts of Pennsylvania in August, 1881. I then removed to New York City,—and served a further apprenticeship to the profession in the office of Walker, Cummins & Hall. I was admitted to practice in New York in February, 1883. I have lived and practiced my profession here without interruption ever since.''

Dix, Edwin A. Has lived in Newark, N. J., since graduation, and practiced law there and in New York. Has spent several summers abroad. In 1889 wrote "A Midsummer Drive through the Pyrenees", published by Putnam in 1890. Is not married nor engaged.

Dix in his year stood first of the five candidates for admission to the New York Bar who received honorary mention on account of their examinations. A correspondent of *Galignani's Messenger* writing from Mustapha, Algiers, mentions Mr. Edwin A. Dix among the participants in a German recently given at the Hotel St. George in that place—Eds.

DODD, W. S. "To give the history of ten years in a letter—how can one do it? And yet, if you look forward to reading these letters as eagerly as I do, every one of them will have its value increased a hundred-fold, for I cannot expect to be present at the Decennial Reunion, or even to see any of my Classmates for a long time to come.

My first five years after leaving Princeton were spent in study in New York, broken by three months of preaching in Minnesota in the summer of 1884. The course was a combined one in Medicine and Theology, and I graduated from Union Theological Seminary in 1884, and from the College of Physicians and Surgeons in 1886. I was married almost immediately after, and sailed with my wife from New York in July of that year. Spending some time in Europe, we reached our home in Turkey in November. From that time until the Spring of 1890 we were busy in our work there, first in learning the Turkish language, and then in general Missionary work. During the last year of that time I was able to devote myself to the medical side of the work, in which I have found more and more pleasure and increasing usefulness, and as a consequence of that I am now here in Vienna.

Desiring to extend much more widely the operations of our Gospel medical work and place it on a more secure basis, we have planned to establish two Dispensaries, one

13

in the city of Cesarea, and one in the neighboring town of Talas, and eventually to have a Hospital is one of these places. To prepare for this, I received permission from our Missionary Society in Boston to come to Germany for a years' study. Last Summer I spent in Heidelberg, and I am now in Vienna where I expect to remain until next Sept. My chief study here is the eye, which branch I shall have to make a specialty in my practice in Turkey. Cesarea, in the heart of Asia Minor, is our headquarters, but we do not confine our work to that city. Either on' horseback or by wagon, we travel over a region of country as large as New York State. With one side of my saddle-bags filled with surgical instruments and a book or two, and the other with drugs and a change of clothing, I am sometimes away from home for weeks at a time.

My wife was Miss Mary L. Carter, of New York City, and we were married at her home June 24, 1886. Edward Mills Dodd came into our household March 30, 1887, and his sister Nellie Feb. 21, 1890. The only "position of honor or trust" that I have filled or expect to fill, is that of missionary. I am very glad of this chance to let the class hear from me, knowing that I shall soon in return hear from them.''

DOUGALL, W. A. "I am still teaching in Newark, N. J., and have charge of a school of about 900 children and sixteen teachers. Have not written any book, but I enjoyed reading Ed Dix's very much. Two years ago I with some other pedagogues made a three-months trip to Europe and visited its famous cities and places. We had a fine time and now look forward with expectation to the time when we can go again. The long Summer vacation is one of the teacher's blessings.

I have two children, a girl, Bessie and a boy, Donald."

DOUGHERTY, A. C. Is a physician, and graduated May, 1882, at College of Physicians and Surgeons, N. Y.— "one of the ten" with prize. Spent eight years as an assistant at St. Michael's Hospital in Newark, and left in Jan., 1890, owing to increase of outside practice.

Was School Commissioner in 1887 and 1888, and is Vice President of Newark Medical Association. Was married in Brooklyn, Dec. 12, 1887 to Miss Mary G. Vose, and has one child, Clarence Vose, born Sept. 27, 1888.

DUFFIELD, H. G. "Since leaving College I have not wandered far from Princeton, for about the middle of September after graduation I went into the Lumber business in Trenton, where I stayed till Aug. 15, 1885 and since then I have been in Princeton as "Assistant to the Treasurer of the College of New Jersey". I might add that in the spring of '86 I found time to "take a course" in Roman Law and play on the Nine, and succeeded in sustaining my reputation as a ball-player, especially in the Yale game, played at Princeton, when I made two "home-runs" off Stagg.

The position I now hold is one of trust, and as the Trustees think one of honor. I have not written a book nor made any great discovery, except that under the system now in vogue, it would be impossible for anyone to grow rich off "Drawbacks". I am not married nor engaged."

DUNN, C. E. "After leaving college I entered Union Theological Seminary, New York City, from which I graduated in '84. I was called to the Presbyterian church

of Hempstead, L. I., in the summer of '84, where I
ministered till the fall of '88, when I was called to the
3rd Pres. Church of Albany N. Y., by whose long-suffer-
ing I am still enabled to enroll myself as an Albanian.   I
was married Aug. 14, 1884, to Miss Emma M. Demarest,
at Plainfield, N. J.   I have three children : William
Parmley, born Aug. 14, 1885, Allen Shoudy, born May 8,
1887, Elizabeth Radley, born Dec. 28, 1888.   I have
filled no special "position of honor or trust", have won no
titles and made no discoveries, but have been plodding
along the path of a glorious mediocrity.   My work in the
ministry has been a success, and my present charge leads
me to indulge a pleasant outlook."

ELLIS, EDWIN M.   "On leaving the Seminary I was
sent to Stevensville, Mont. by the Board of Home
Missions, and have remained there ever since.   My occupation is that of a Presbyterian minister and an editor, having been running a paper, "The Light of the Valley", over
two years.   I have organized and built three churches,
and re-officered another—all in this Valley— also organized several Sunday Schools and the Missoula County Sunday School Association, of which I have been Secretary
since its foundation nearly three years ago.   Have received into the church about 115 members.

I was married July 28, 1883 in Amherst N. H. to
Miss Lilla M. Prince and have two children—Wilder
Prince, born Dec. 24, 1886 and Nina Pauline, born May
25, 1889."

FARR, T. H. P.   "Immediately on leaving College
I entered the banking office of Fisk & Hatch, where
I remained for nearly two years.   On April 1, 1883 Mr.

W. Howard Gilder (brother of Ed Gilder of our class, now deceased) and myself organized the present banking and brokerage firm of Gilder, Farr & Co., 31-33 Broad Street, N. Y.

I was married April 14, 1884 to Miss Maria W. Harding of Philadelphia. We will take great pleasure in introducing to any that may call our eldest son, the "Class Cup boy", T. H. Powers Farr Jr., born Feb. 21st, 1885, our daughter, Georgiana Harding, born May 30th, 1887, and our youngest son, Barclay Harding, born Sept, 6th 1890. I think that after meeting this noble array of children my Classmates will agree that more honor and credit will rebound to the Class through them, than through any book that might be written or any discovery that might be made by the most brilliant of the Sons of '81.''

FISK, P. "I am a member of the firm of Harvey Fisk & Sons, dealers in Government bonds and investment securities.

I was married the 8th of October, 1882, at Woodstock, Vermont, to Miss Mary L. Chapman. We have two children, viz.: Edith C., born April 30, 1884, and Dorothy, born August 8, 1888.''

FLICK, W. J. "I have been located permanently in Wilkes Barre, Pa. since '82, where I opened an office and have followed my profession of Civil and Mining Engineer ever since. On Feb. 1st left home with my mother on a trip to California, where we are visiting a brother of mine.

I am still single, though on a sort of "still-hunt" for a wife, and am ready to fall as soon as I meet *the* one.''

FOWLER, W. "After leaving College I read law at Washington, where I was admitted to the bar, and since then I have been practicing "Patent Law" as a specialty. I came to New York Dec. '87, was admitted here, and have been trying to eke out a living by practicing my profession in this city. Am not married nor engaged."

FROST, G. C. "Pastor of the First Presbyterian Church Three Rivers, Mich. Married here July 25, 1888, to Miss Claudia Bennett. Have one son, George Antes, born Sept. 15, 1890."

GILL, C. R. JR. No report.

GLEDHILL, F. "My career since leaving college has not been of a startling character. After having passed the required three year's course in a law office, I was in June, 1884, admitted to practice law in New Jersey, and since then have followed that profession. In the fall of 1884, with Charley Danforth, I visited England, and spent a month viewing various places of historic interest. A portion of the summer of 1888 I spent in California ; and on Aug. 16th I was married to Miss Florence E. Perine, in Fruit Vale, a suburb of Oakland, Cal. We have no children living.

Up to the present writing my desire for political preferment has been gratified by an election as one of the Commissioners of Public Instruction at the last municipal election in Paterson, N. J."

GOSMAN, C. N. No report. Cowan writes that "Dominie" is City Clerk of Butte City, Montana.

GROVE, J. R. 2. "Have engaged in a variety of occupations.

3. Single.

4. Sorry I have been unable to accomplish anything to the credit of '81."

HAMMOND, E. P. T. Is practicing law in Snow Hill, Md., and still remains single.

HARLAN, R. D. Entered the Princeton Theological Seminary in the autumn of 1882, and took the regular three years course and one post-graduate year. Was ordained April 1, 1886 and installed Pastor of the First Presbyterian Church, New York City, succeeding the Rev. Wm. M. Paxton, now of the Theological Seminary at Princeton. After four and a half years work in that parish resigned his charge Nov. 1, 1890, and shortly after sailed for Germany to pursue special studies at the University of Berlin in the "Biblical Theology" of the New Testament and in Church History under Weiss and Harnack. Expects to remain in Berlin about a year longer.

Was married June 5, 1889 to Mrs. Margeret Prouty Swift in Geneva, New York. In May 1889 was elected by the General Assembly a member of the Board of Church Erection, and the same year was chosen to fill a vacancy in the Board of Directors of the Princeton Theological Seminary.

HARRISON, G. "After trying various portions of the Old and New worlds, I have settled in England, as I find the good people are less hard on us poor drones than they are under the Star Spangled Banner. [The capitals are ours.—Eds.] I was married March 19, 1888, at Thomasville, Ga., to Mrs. F. A. Marquand, and have one child, a boy, born April 3, 1889. Before closing I should like to add my humble tribute of respect and affection to the memory of our friend David Haynes, whom my good fortune placed next me in class; and I shall esteem it the greatest honor if you will allow my name to be added to the resolutions the class will pass as a memorial to him.''

DAVID ADAMS HAYNES died of peritonitis in New York City, Dec. 8th, 1890 in the thirty-first year of his age.

Probably the death of no one of its members could have been felt more keenly by the Class. Both as a man, and as the recognized official head of the Class Haynes was in a double sense representative. Socially he filled a place in all of the various ''sets'' into which a Class naturally divides, intellectually he showed more perhaps than any other member the stimulating and beneficial results of college training, and it was in recognition of this fact that he was elected to deliver the Master's Oration. His character was a rare combination of gentleness and strength, a high type of Christian manhood pervaded by true religious feeling, yet entirely free from cant—a character that won the respect of all. Those that have heard him speak of his Mother may divine the unseen influence that shaped his life.

Haynes' last illness was a very brief one—Friday, the 5th he was at his office, but went home early ; on Saturday his symptoms became alarming, and on Sunday it was decided that the trouble was peritonitis and that an immediate operation was necessary. After this was performed it became apparent that there was no hope and death followed at one o'clock on Monday, the 8th.

The following is taken from the *New York Tribune*, of Dec. 9th, 1890 : ''He was born in June, 1860, at Harrisburg, Penn., and received his early education in Washington, D. C. He was graduated from Princeton in 1881 with high honors, and in 1884 he was selected by the Faculty of the College to deliver the Master's Oration, receiving at that time the Master's degree. Having studied law at the Columbian University, Washington, where he received his degree of LL. B., he came to New York in 1883 and at the time of his death was a member of the law firm of Morse, Haynes & Wensley, whose headquarters are in the Astor Building, No. 10 Wall St.

Mr. Haynes's fine oratorical abilities soon brought him into prominence, and he had already acquired considerable reputation both as an erudite lawyer and special pleader. While in Washington he acted as superintendent of the Sunday-school attached to the Kendal Memorial Chapel, and he was also a Trustee and Secretary of the Board of Bishop's College. In New York he served a term in the Excise Board and was a member of the University Club and chairman of the class committee, which next year will present Princeton College with a set of plaster casts. He was unmarried and had a wide circle of friends and acquaintances.''

The following expression of the sorrow of the Class was prepared by the Committee appointed at the Decennial Reunion :

The Class of 1881 of Princeton College at this its Decennial Reunion desires to express its profound sense of the loss which it has sustained in the recent death of its President, David Adams Haynes.

As Junior Orator, as Lynde Debater and as Master's Orator he had represented the Class before the college world with honor and success. In his chosen profession, the law, he had at the time of his death achieved a distinction which marked him as exceptionally fitted for the highest rewards that can fall to eminent ability coupled with faithful diligence. But his loss is felt most keenly because of the place he had won in the hearts of his classmates. His love and devotion to the Class which delighted to do him honor were equalled only by the deep affection felt for him by all those whose memories could look back on four years of college friendship and who for ten years had followed his career with sympathy for his struggles and joy for his successes.

J. LEVERETT MOORE
JOHN O. H. PITNEY
W. A. ROBINSON

Princeton, N. J.   Committee.
June 8, 1891.

HILLHOUSE, J. S. "The ten years of my history since graduation are to be accounted for as follows :— three years in Princeton Theological Seminary, two at Ringgold, Ga., preaching, and five at the same occupation at Cartersville, Ga., 50 miles from Atlanta on a direct line from Chattanooga. Married to Miss Belle Boaz at Calhoun, Ga., March 1, 1888 and welcomed a son, Walter Boaz, Jan. 29, 1889, and another, Joseph Newton, Feb. 25, 1891."

HUBBARD, J. D. "In the fall of 1885 I was admitted to the Bar and have ever since been occupied with the duties of my profession.

I was married to Miss Janet Watson, April 19th, 1888.

As '81 men are few and far between in this locality, I hope to find a big majority of the Class at the Decennial Reunion."

HUDNUT, A. M. "Since the last Class Record there has been little change in my affairs. I am still in the same business—Banking, and doing fairly well. I have

22

not yet "domesticated" any one of the "Recording Angels" to which Robert Louis Stephenson refers, but as I have been spoken for by the daughter of one of our Classmates, age three years, I consider the question of matrimony settled."

INGHAM, W. "I hardly know what to say in regard to my life for the last ten years, so little has happened to make it eventful. I am still a would be coal-baron, am not married, or even engaged, and that sums up my last ten years. I hope to have the pleasure of seeing you in June, and pledging the health of '81."

JACKSON, P. N. "After leaving college I studied law for about a year in the office of my uncle, Schuyler B. Jackson, in Newark, and also attended lectures at the Columbia Law School in New York. On July 1, 1882 I entered the employ of the Newark Electric Light and Power Co. as Assistant Secretary, and have continued with the Company ever since in the various capacities of Sec., Sec. and Treas., Treas. and Manager, Vice Pres. and Manager, the last of which I now occupy. I am also Sec. and Treas. of the Newark Schuyler Electric Light Co., and the Thompson Electric Co., both operated by the Newark E. L. and P. Co. I am an officer in a number of different enterprises, viz.: Treas. of the Holbrook Printing Co., and of Williams & Co., a book-binding concern, and Pres. of the Essex Land Co.

On November 5th, 1884 I was married in Germantown, Pa., to Miss Margeret Atlee, and have four children— Nannie Nye, born Aug. 11, 1885, Edith Atlee, born Oct. 6, 1886, Frederick Wolcott, 3rd, born Feb. 30, 1888, and Margeret Atlee, born Nov. 11, 1890.

K IMBALL, A. L. "After graduation, having taken the Experimental Science Fellowship, I spent a year in Princeton doing graduate work in physics, and the following June was appointed Fellow in Physics in Johns Hopkins University in Baltimore. After a year devoted to special study I was appointed Chief Assistant in charge of some experiments which were carried on under a special appropriation made by the United States Government to fix the standard of electrical resistance. These experiments were under the general direction of Prof. Rowland of the Johns Hopkins University, and absorbed nearly all my time and attention for a year. A report of them has been prepared and will doubtless be published in course of time.

In June 1884 I received the degree of Doctor of Philosophy, and was appointed Associate in Physics in the Johns Hopkins University. Since then my work has gradually grown, so that I have had charge of all the undergraduate work in Physics and partial direction of the graduate students also. In 1886-7 a large Physical Laboratory was built, and I was much occupied in attending to the proper execution of the plans. In June 1888 I was made Associate Professor of Physics, and held this position up to last May when I was elected Professor of Physics in Amherst College, with the promise of a new Physical Laboratory to be begun at once.

I was married to Miss Lucilla Scribner, Augusth 25, 1884, and we have had three children, all boys :—Arthur Livingstone born February 22, 1886, William Scribner born August 28, 1887, and Stanley Fisher born January 6, 1890. The last little one died very suddenly in July 1890, when only six months old.

The only things I have published besides various book

reviews and notices, are two papers which appeared in the *Electrical World*, one on Electromagnetic Radiation and the other on Electrical Units, and a little book in the Riverside Science Series treating in a somewhat popular manner of the "Physical Properties of Gases". The book has been favorably reviewed, but judging from its sale I fear that the rays of glory which it may be destined to shed on the Class will be very mild indeed."

Kimball modestly omits to mention that Pres. Gates of Amherst referred to him as "one of the foremost scientific men of the country".—*Eds.*

THOMAS D. KING died at his home in Springfield, Ohio, December 23rd 1888, at the age of twenty-nine.

After leaving Princeton he began the study of medicine and graduated with "distinguished merit" from the Univ. of Pa. in 1885. He was greatly interested in mission work, and after practicing in Springfield for about a year, offered himself as a Medical Missionary to the Pres. Board of Foreign Missions. Before he had been assigned to his field, a tumor began to manifest itself in the cavity of the right eye, against which all the efforts of medical skill were of no avail. For the last two years of his life he suffered excruciating pain, his strength being constantly wasted by the disease.

The *Springfield Gazette* said of him: "In quiet deeds of kindness to the poor, in words of cheer to the despondent and struggling, in labors to lead the sinful to repentance and salvation *   *   *   * he filled his years with usefulness and scattered blessings with lavish hand at every step of his life."

KIRK, J. L.

"2. Law.

3. I'll none of it.

4. No.

5. I have none.

6. Perhaps."

We learn through Vanderburgh that Kirk has sold his brewery, and has decided to enter Columbia Law School.

KNOWLES, E. R.   No report.

LANDON, F. G.   "Since July 1881 my life has been the same as any business man's and very uneventful. My business has been the same, viz., importing Ladies Dress Goods, or as we are called simply—Importers. I am still single with poor prospects for a change of life."

LANG, L. J.   "Soon after graduation, I became a reporter upon the *Philadelphia Times*. I found within six weeks that I was growing so rich in the Quaker City, that I decided to make a strike in New York. For six months I was attached to the *Times* in that city as reporter. Being summoned home by the illness of my mother, I was for a year news editor of the Elmira *Daily Advertiser*. In the spring of 1883, I returned to New York and became connected with the *Daily Graphic* in a semi-editorial capacity. Not long after, I accepted a place upon the staff of the *New York World*. I represented that journal, in part, at the Presidential Convention of 1884, and throughout the campaign was a gleaner of political nuggets for the columns of that paper. Later I became the Albany correspondent of the *World*. In August, '88, I went upon the staff of the *N. Y. Press*, as a political writer. I followed this line of work through the campaign of that year, and in 1889 was promoted to my present position of Washington correspondent of that paper.

Dec. 24, 1883, I was married to Miss Clara Osborne Terhune, of Brooklyn. A son, Frederick Lyford, was born in Brooklyn, May 14, 1885, and a daughter, Clara Louise Cushing, in Washington, March 13, 1891."

LONEY, F. "I followed the law in the East, and then went West, where corner lots have been receiving most of my attention. I am still unmarried. At present I expect to be with you at the Decennial Reunion, and am expecting great pleasure from meeting so many old friends of former years."

LOUCKS, Z. K., JR. "Immediately after leaving College I returned to my home in York, Pa., and for fifteen months devoted my time exclusively to the Real Estate business, and the management of manufacturing industries in which my family was then engaged. Having determined upon the law as my profession I registered under the Hon. John Gibson of York, and upon his elevation to the Judiciary was handed over to the tender mercies of his uncle, the late Hon. Robert J. Fisher, under whose preceptorship I remained for more than a year. I then decided to locate in Philadelphia and with this end in view entered the law office of the Hon. George Junkin, of Presbyterian fame, and continued my legal studies under his direction until my admission to the Bar, Feb. 5, 1887. Since then I have been actively and industriously engaged in the prosecution of my chosen profession. I enjoy a good clientage and aside from the cases which generally fall to the lot of the practitioner, I have been retained in several important causes involving complex questions and much money.

I have neither wife nor children to beautify and adorn my home, or to share my joys and tribulations as I am hastening down the corridor of time. Moreover I am not engaged, so far as I know of, but am of a marriageable age, and at present matrimonial stock is at a discount with me."

MC ALPIN, H. M. "The winter after leaving college I attended the Columbia Law School, and spent the following winter in Athens, Ga., at the Law School of the University of Georgia. The next fall I returned to Savannah, commenced the practice of law, and during the first year met with such success that my health began to fail from the mental and physcial strain, and the following summer I went to Europe on a vacation of about four months. Upon my return to Savannah I was married in November to Miss Claudia Thomas of Athens, Ga., and continued to practice law for two years after my marriage. On July 6th, 1887, my little daughter, Claudia Thomas was born, and shortly after I concluded to break up my practice and cast in my lot among the "Athenians". This change was accomplished the latter part of October, and on the 6th of November my wife died. I remained in Athens until the latter part of the next year, when I sailed for Europe, and travelled in Spain, Africa and Russia, during which time I wrote a number of articles for newspapers in America. In November, 1889, I started the practice of my profession again in Savannah, and in October of the next year the accumulation of private and professional work compelled me to form a partnership with Mr. W. P. La Roche.

I have partially compiled a Law Book, which as yet has not seen the light of day. I was a delegate to the

Gubernatorial Convention of 1888, but have kept out of politics ever since and hope to for the future.''

McCoy, W. I. "In Sept. '79, I entered the class of 1882 at Harvard University and graduated with it in due course. The summer and fall of 1882 I spent in Europe, and entered the Harvard Law School in Sept. '83, in the class of 1886, with which class I graduated. I was admitted to practice law in the courts of the State of New York Dec. '86, and have continued in practice ever since. I was married Oct. 17, 1888, to Miss Kate Philbrick Baldwin in New York City. We have a son, Percy Beach McCoy, 2nd, who was born Dec. 11, 1889.''

McCune, A. "I read law at Rockville, Ind., for one year after leaving Nassau Hall. The following year I went to the Ann Arbor Law School, but did not graduate. Came to Minneapolis in March, '83, and went into the office of Cross, Hicks & Carleton for one year. In Oct. '83, passed the examination for admission to the bar in this State, opened an office and went in for fame alone. Soon got tired of trying to find it in that way, and in Nov. '84, formed a partnership with Edwin S. Slater, an Oberlin graduate. We practiced under the firm name of Slater & McCune till June, '87, when I came into the office of Edward M. Johnson, on a sort of partnership basis so far as the income of the office goes. I was married Oct. 20, 1886, at Lima, New York, to Miss Clara A. McNair. We have two children—Clara, three years old, and Mary, six months ; both fine girls, and the pride of the household.''

McDermont, H. "When I left New Jersey I started studying law in Dayton, O., was admitted by the Supreme

Court in June 1883, and have since been a struggling lawyer.

I was married to Miss Rosalie B. Thruston at Cumberland, Md., March 21st, 1882, and have five children living; my eldest boy, Clarke, died when ten months old. My oldest girl, Rosalie Thruston, was born June 2nd, 1883, my second daughter, Katherine Winters, on March 22nd, 1886, the twins, Thruston and Eliza, on March 14, 1888, and the last and best, Chapman, April 24th, 1890.

I am doing pretty well for my country, don't you think?''

CHARLES McKEE died of brain fever near Lewistown, Pa., July 31st, 1882, in the thirtieth year of his age.

After graduating he studied law in Lewistown. While working in the harvest field he was suddenly taken ill, and ten days later died of brain fever brought on by exposure to the sun.

THOMAS EDWARD McLURE was born August 29, 1858, and died April 27, 1889.

He was a lawyer by profession, a close student, and rapidly advancing to success. He was married Jan. 20, 1886, to Miss Maud Reynolds, of Rendalia, Ala. He left a son, still living, born Dec. 20, 1888, named Thomas John McLure.

McMURDY, W. S. '' The degree of M. D. was conferred on me by the College of Physicians and Surgeons, Sept., 1885. On account of my father's illness I remained at my home in Delhi, N. Y., until Feb., 1886, when I returned to this city. During the spring and early summer I was in the employ of a large chemical house ; from Aug., 1886, to Mar. 1887, ambulance surgeon at Bellevue

Hospital; then to Dec. 1887, junior house physician at N. Y. Skin and Cancer Hospital; and since have been in private practice in New York. Was married Oct. 23, 1889, to Miss Fannie Maccabe, in New York. One bright son has been added to the syndicate—William George, born July 29, 1890.''

MANIERRE, C. E. "I have continued in the practice of the law since my admission to the Bar in 1883. For the last two years my brother and I have had our offices together and jointly have been enticing the coy dollar in our direction. In 1884 I became deeply impressed by the mischief which results from the liquor traffic and determined to take a hand in suppressing the business. The next year I joined the Prohibition Party and since then have given a large share of my time and thought to that subject.

My vacations have usually been spent camping and fishing in the Adirondack Mountains. When I lift my eyes to the matrimonial heavens so many brilliant stars dazzle the sight that if my "bright particular star" is among them I am as yet unable to discern her.''

MINOR, G. W. No report.

MONROE, R. G. "I am practicing law and have been so engaged since 1884. After leaving college I studied for a year in Philadelphia at the Law School there, came to New York in the fall of 1882, took my degree in the Columbia Law School after a year's study and then read for a year in an office before I was admitted to practice.

I am neither married nor engaged; nor have I written a book, made a discovery, or done anything to make my Class proud of me.''

MOORE, J. L. "My time since graduation has been spent in teaching and study, partly in Princeton, partly in Baltimore at the Johns Hopkins University. The year '81-2 I remained in Princeton and pursued certain graduate courses. I was then appointed Tutor of Latin in the College and held the position three years. In 1885 I came to Baltimore and entered the Johns Hopkins University with which I have remained connected up to the present time, having been a Fellow in 1887-8, and Instructor in Latin, 1886, 1888-9. I received the degree of Ph. D. last February, and have just been elected Associate Professor of Latin in Vassar College. The only thing I have written for publication is the dissertation presented for my degree, which will appear in the current volume of the American Journal of Philology. I am engaged to be married."

LYMAN G. MOREY was drowned in some lake in Michigan during the summer of 1888. His boat upset in a storm.

MUNN, C. A. "I came into the office of the "Scientific American" January 1, 1883, and have been connected with the publication of the paper ever since that time. I am unmarried."

MYERS, S. H. "2. Present occupation, Cotton Merchant: up to '85, Dry Goods, Wholesale.

3. Married June 25th, 1890 to Miss Nona Stern.

4. None worthy of mention."

OLDS, J. G. No report. Is a lawyer and recently left Newark, N. J. for one of the new Western states. When last heard from he was with a party of prospectors among the Cascade Mountains, and intended to return to Tacoma, Washington, after the trip. He was married in 1889.

ORR, F. J. "'The first two years after leaving College I spent in teaching at Sing Sing, N. Y. and Oxford, Pa. I then entered the United Presbyterian Seminary at Allegheny, Pa., and graduated in '85 among the first. I did mission work for two years in Ohio, Kansas, Arkansas, Pennsylvania, and Iowa, and at last settled at Coulterville, Ill., as pastor ; but health failing because of climatic change, I was compelled to resign. I soon began mission work again, and on regaining health settled as pastor in Mulberry, Mo., in January '90. I also have charge of a mission field at Amoret, which has increased 20 in number during the last year.

September 1st, 1885 I was married to Miss Adena I. Lawrence of New Jersey at Wellington, Kansas, and June 21, '86 Adena Esther was born, November 1, '88 Lawrence."

PITNEY, J. O. H. "I am still pegging away at the Law at the old stand, and have thus far had success and good fortune far beyond my expectations, and quite equal to my loftiest ambition.

I was married in Newark, N. J., January 15th, 1890 to Miss Roberta A. Ballantine, and have no children.

I have occupied no public position, written no book, and beyond what I have stated, have done nothing to cause '81's pride in me to be puffed up."

PORTER, H. C. No report. He taught for several years at Brown's, a prominent school for boys in Philadelphia. Then, as we are informed, married a rich wife, quit work, and is now living abroad.

PRESTON, W. W. "A member of the Maryland bar, took the degree of LL. B. at the Maryland University Law School in May, 1883. Was elected to the

General Assembly of Maryland in 1888, re-elected in 1890, and served as Chairman of the Committees on the Judiciary and Claims. Am W. Master of the lodge at Bel Air of Ancient Free and Accepted Masons.

Am unmarried and without any immediate prospect of a change."

E. DUNBAR PRICE died in New York City Dec. 4, 1890 in his thirty-second year.

The following details are gathered from the "Baltimore American" of that date : By the death of his grandfather, Elon Dunbar, in 1877, Price inherited an income of $15,000 a year, which shortly afterwards was more than doubled by the death of his grandmother and sister, and finally increased to $42,000. Upon inheriting this fortune Price launched out into various extravagances, kept a racing stable, and ran horses.

In 1881 he married Miss Sarah C. Burton of Philadelphia and the wedding was one of the events of the social season.

REID, A. T. "I am still an employee of the Colorado National Bank, of Denver. In fact this day's work completes seven years of service here. I can't honestly say 'Blessed be the tie that binds' me to Colorado, as I would rather live in New York City than anywhere else. I suppose you will have a great time in June. I had planned to attend, but will fail to connect. Last summer I was called unexpectedly to Boston by the illness of my father, which resulted fatally. As we get older our enthusiasm leaves us to some extent, but I have still all my affection for Princeton, as sundry bets on her foot--ball and base-ball teams will attest."

WILLIAM HUGH RENDALL died of consumption at

Lincoln University, Pa., October 22, 1882, in his twenty-first year.

RICKETTS, L. D. "I have been unfortunate in failing to meet Classmates in recent years, and visiting Princeton scarcely brings back recollections unalloyed, for one is rendered somewhat nervous and exasperated by the presence of a crowd of strange, beardless *boys*, who somehow seem to have usurped the rights that once belonged to the *men* that we were ten or fourteen years ago.

I am by occupation a Mine Superintendent and Mining Engineer. Since leaving College I have been engaged as follows: June-Sept. '81, Topographical surveying in New York state; Sept. '81-June '83, pursuing my studies at the School of Science in Princeton and doing field work near Leadville, Col., in order to obtain the degree of Doctor of Science (D. Sc.), which in due time I received from Princeton; July '83-March '85, Surveyor and Mining Engineer for the Morning and Evening Star Mines, at Leadville, Col.; March '85-Dec. '86, Superintendent of the Gipsey Maid Consolidated Mining Company at Silverton, Col.; Dec. '86-April '87, Mining Engineer at Leadville, Col.; April '87-Nov. '90 Geologist and Mining Engineer for the Territory of Wyoming; Nov. '90 Mining Engineer for the Copper Queen and Commercial Mining Companies, with headquarters in New York City.

I have published the dissertation for my degree of D. Sc. upon "The Ores of Leadville and their Modes of Occurrence as illustrated in the Morning and Evening Star Mines", New York, May 1883, and the "Biennial Reports of the Territorial Geologist to the Governor of Wyoming", Cheyenne, 1887 and 1889. I am neither married nor engaged."

ROBBINS, CARROLL. "I spent a year in Princeton after graduation, as Fellow in Mathematics, and then taught Mathematics a year in a private school in Baltimore. In September 1883 I began the study of law in Trenton, N. J. During the College-year 1884-5 I acted as Tutor of Mathematics at Princeton. The next winter I was a student in the Columbia College Law School, was admitted to the Bar, November, 1886 and since that time have been practicing law in Trenton. I have had a fair amount of business and it seems to be on the increase.

I was married October 12th, 1887 to Edna Thompson (Oberlin '83) at Urbana, Ohio. The Rev. George L. Van Alen performed the ceremony, and I can recommend him to any of my classmates who may need such services in the future.

After careful consideration I am unable to think of anything that I have done to make my class feel proud of me."

ROBERTS, E. G. No report. Still lives in Columbus, O., but is too rich to do much business. Ad Rogers saw him three years ago at a Princeton Alumni Dinner in Cincinnati, and McDermont testifies to the fact of his still being alive.

ROBERTS, W. H. "I have no report to make further than the one made at our five-year reunion. [Billy probably refers to the Triennial Record in which we find "No report" under his name.—Eds.] I am still engaged in the banking business at the old stand. Am not married or even engaged, hence have no family to speak of."

ROBINSON, W. A. "Since leaving college I have lived two years in Germany, six months at Marietta, O., two years and a half at Allegheny, one year at Lewisburg,

Pa., and am now in my third year at South Bethlehem, Pa. (It is true that in the above statement the sum of the parts does not equal the whole, but I am not writing for the special benefit of our mathematicians.) In Germany I was a student of Classical Philology, chiefly Greek; at Marietta and Lewisburg, I filled temporarily the Greek chairs in Marietta College and Bucknell University; at Allegheny, I coached boys for Princeton, Yale and Harvard—two of my boys graduated this year from Princeton; and at South Bethlehem, I am Professor of Greek in Lehigh University, and also Secretary of the Faculty—an office which bears more *onus* than honor.

I was married in Brooklyn, November 26, 1888 to Miss Anna Green MacLaren. A Princeton Trustee assisted in the ceremony, my best man was from '86 and my ushers included four '81 men and one each from '83, '86, '90, and '91. I have no candidate for future foot-ball— or classical—honors at Princeton, but Miss Elizabeth Mac-Laren Robinson, born February 8, 1890, will be taught to look upon the Orange and Black as her own colors."

ROBINSON, W. F. "After leaving college, I entered the Albany Medical College at Albany, N. Y. graduating in 1884. I practiced medicine in Albany, being associated with my brother-in-law, Dr. J. S. Delavan, and at his death continued practice alone until June '87, when I went to Europe in order to study a specialty. It seemed clear to me that the future of medicine lay in specialism and I chose for my own, the subject of nervous diseases, for which I had always had a special fondness. I pursued the study of my specialty in all the principal clinics of Europe, finding unusual advantages in Vienna where I obtained the position of Voluntary Assistant in the two

large nervous Clinics and also in the Clinic for the In-
sane. I became much interested in the subject of hypnot-
ism and saw all that was done in this curious science, both
at Paris and at Nancy. I am convinced that there is a
great deal in it, but there is no probability of its ever
coming into use for therapeutic purposes, on account of
the uncertainty of its action, the attendant dangers and
numerous other reasons. It will probably always remain
what it now is—a scientific curiosity.

When I returned home in August 1890, I spent a
short time in visiting and in October of the same year I
reopened my office in Albany for the practice of my
specialty which is my occupation at the present time. I
am neither married nor engaged."

RODGERS, A S. "The year after graduation I taught
in the Miami Classical School, near Cincinnati. In the
fall of '82 I began the study of law at my home, and
finishing my studies at the Law School of Cincinnati, was
admitted to the Bar in the spring of '85. Since then, as
is the case with most young lawyers, my occupation and
business has been more or less. The only positions of
honor and trust that I have filled are those of Judge of
Elections in my ward, and god-father to MacDermont's boy
—a twin. I have written no books, made no discoveries
and the only reason I can give why my Class should be
proud of me is that in my profession I have charged all
that the traffic would bear, and have paid my honest debts.
I am still unmarried and prospects are *nil.*"

ROSEBERRY, F. M. "Immediately after my graduation from College, I studied law in my brother's office in
Belvidere, N. J., until November, when I cast in my lot
with the West and entered the Law Department of the

University of Iowa, from which I graduated in '83. On my return to Iowa after a visit to my former home in New Jersey, I opened a law office in Lemars, Plymouth Co., Iowa, where I have practiced my chosen profession and where I expect to reside in the future.

In September, 1885 I married Miss Della M. Page and we have one child, a boy, Clarence Depue, now four years old. The world has dealt kindly with me and mine ; I am doing well, enjoying good health, and would be pleased to meet any of my Classmates at my home. I have not seen more than four or five members of '81 since the day we graduated.''

ADRIAN SCHARFF died at Nashville, Tenn., Nov. 2, 1890, aged 30 years.

"When his father lay dying he called to his bedside his oldest son, Adrian, then scarcely nine years old, and gave him a charge concerning the entire family. He was to care for and comfort his mother, and be an example and a father to his younger brothers and sisters. Into this inheritance of care and responsibility he entered manfully, and while life lasted his first anxiety seemed to be to fulfil to the uttermost this trust.

He graduated from Columbia Law School in 1884, and practiced in the local courts of Newark, until in 1888 he became examiner of claims and auditor for the Fidelity and Casualty Insurance Co. of New York. He was employed as their attorney, with large responsibility, until the time of his death at Nashville, Tenn., where he had opened an office for the company, with the intention of making his home in that city.

He was active in church work, particularly among the young. While working in this direction he organized a Lend-a-Hand Club, met with the boys evenings, taught them how to carry on their club meetings profitably, entertained them in his home. Their lives to-day are showing how truly they prized his example and his lessons in manly living."

SCHMIDT, G. S. "I spent two years in Philadelphia reading law in the office of Atty-Genl. Brewster, and attending lectures in the Law Department of the Univ. of Pa. I was admitted to the Bar in June 1884 and have been practicing ever since. About two years ago I purchased a half interest in a manufacturing plant having for its object the heating of houses with steam or hot water, and also the manufacture and sale of Boilers, Radiators, etc., which business is carried on concurrently with my practice of the law. I have also been somewhat interested in politics, and for the past five years have been Chairman of the Republican County Committee, and represented the 19th Cong. Dist. of this State as Delegate to the Republican National Convention of 1888. I have been for some time a Director in one of our National Banks, and as a Director in our Street Railway Co., keep a watchful eye on the elusive nickel as it disappears in the slot. I am contemplating the matrimonial step shortly after our Reunion in June."

"Dot" was married June 16, '91 to Miss Mary Richardson Small in York, Pa.—Eds.

SCHNEIDEMAN, T. B. "Studied medicine after leaving Princeton. Upon graduation was resident physician in the Philadelphia Hospital for one year. Engaged in general practice for a few years, but have limited my practice for the last three years to diseases of the eye. Am instructor in Ophthalmology, Philadelphia Polyclinic Col-

lege for Graduates in Medicine, assistant surgeon to Wills'
Eye Hospital, oculist to St. Christopher's Hospital for
Children, and editor of the "Transactions of the Philadelphia County Medical Society". Am not married nor
engaged."

SCRIBNER, A. H. "I fear I have little to add to my
report in the Triennial Record. I am still a member of
the firm of Charles Scribners' Sons, Publishers, 743-5
Broadway, N. Y. and my work in connection with it is
most interesting and absorbing. Otherwise the ten years
have been comparatively uneventful. My interest in
Princeton is keen as ever and contrary to the general
prophecy I find that the old college friendships have only
strengthened with time. I am neither married nor engaged."

SCRIBNER, H. S. "The year after leaving college I
spent in Saratoga teaching in a private school. I next
taught the classics at the Sedgwick Institute, Gt. Barring-
ton, Mass., for three years. In the fall of 1885, I entered the Johns Hopkins Univ. as a graduate student, and
for three years pursued courses in Greek, Latin, Sanskrit
and other subjects. In July, 1888, I went abroad, and
put in six months' study at Göttingen, with some travel
before and after. I came home and spent the following
year teaching Latin at Lake Forest, Ill. Last summer I
accepted a call to the chair of Greek in the Western
University of Pa., at Allegheny, and occupy that position
at present. I am engaged to be married."

SELHEIMER, H. C. "The first year after leaving
college I passed at my old home, after which I went to
Philadelphia and read law in the office of Rufus E. Shap-
ley, Esq. I was admitted to the bar in Philadelphia May

3d, 1884. In May, 1885, I came to Birmingham, Ala., where I first entered upon the practice of my profession, and where I have since resided. After considerable struggle I have met with fair success, and am permanently located. I am still single and without any present intention of changing this state of supposed blessedness. It would give me unbounded pleasure to be present at the Decennial Reunion, and you may be sure I shall make an effort to be there.''

ROBERT R. SHELLABARGER died of typhoid fever in Washington D. C. January 10, 1889 in the thirtieth year of his age.

He was a member of the bar of the District of Columbia and junior member of the firm of Shellabarger & Wilson, in which his father was the senior partner. He was regarded as a young lawyer of exceptional brilliancy and promise. He was married June 17, 1886 to Miss Sara ——— and was the father of two children—Mildred, born March 12, died July 13, 1887 and Samuel Shellabarger Jr., born May 18, 1888.

SINCLAIR, G. M. "In my case the bald facts will, I think, suffice, saving the valuable space of the Record for those who can spin more thrilling yarns. After taking my degree of M. E., I spent three years in the practice of that profession at the Midvale Steel Works in Philadelphia. I then went abroad for over a year to regain my somewhat impaired health. On my return I spent two years in the Ordnance Works of the Bethlehem Iron Co. Am now back at Midvale. Have not startled the world by any wonderful inventions or marvellous piece of engineering, nor have I startled my friends by getting married, or even engaged.''

SKINNER, J. B. "I hardly know what my occupation is. The enclosed cards, etc., will give you an idea of some of the matters I am interested in. There are some half-dozen others, but these are the main ones. I practiced law up to two years ago, as one of the attorneys of the B. & O. R. R. Co., and other large corporations, and think I can say with all due modesty, I had the best practice of any lawyer of my age (or ten years my senior) in Chicago. Married Feb. 1, 1887, in Chicago. Wife's maiden name, Jane Lapham Barnard. No children. [Miss B. was niece of late U. S. Senator Lapham, of New York.—Eds.] Don't know of anything that would make the class proud of me, unless they should consider it something of a feat to get together somewhere between ¼ and ½ million dollars in a short space of time."

It appears from "the enclosed cards etc" that Bonner, besides being a real estate operator on no small scale, is Pres. and Treas. of the "Hercules Iron Works", Pres. and Treas. of the "Chemical Automatic Sprinkler Co". *and* President of "The W. C. Coup Enchanted Rolling Palaces, Eden Musée, Aquarium and Auditorium".

Roll on, ye W. C. Coup Enchanted Palaces—roll ! —*Byron.*

SMALL, E. H. "In 1885 I took the degree of M. D. in the Medical Department of the University of Pennsylvania. From July '85 to July '86 I served as Resident Physician and Surgeon in the West Penn Hospital in Pittsburgh. Then I spent a year abroad walking the hospitals in London, Berlin and Vienna, and incidentally travelling about. On my return I settled in Allegheny City, Pa., where I remained for two years and a half, but not liking my location there I bought a lot in Pittsburgh and built a residence with offices in which I hope to live and die. I hold the position of Lecturer on the Diseases of Children at the West Penn Medical College and have charge of the same department in the Dispensary connected with that institution. I am also Assistant Gynæcologist to the Pittsburgh Free Dispensary. I have written a number of papers for different medical societies of which I am a member, some of which have been published.

I am not married nor have I any immediate prospect in that direction."

STANTON, L. H. No news of recent date. "Jack" Fowler met him in Washington about six years ago on his wedding tour. He had married a young lady from New Orleans and was on his way home, which at that time was Morris, Minn.

STRONG, W. N. No report. Left St. Paul some time ago. Married in Washington D. C. by the Rev. R. D. Harlan, and is now living in Scranton, Pa.

SYMMES, F. R. "Since leaving college I spent two years in teaching school, three years in study at the Princeton Theological Seminary and five years in the Gospel Ministry. On May 13th, 1886 I was ordained to the ministry by the Presbytery of West Jersey and also installed pastor of the Fairfield Presbyterian Church at Fairton, N. J. After remaining there nearly four years, I was installed pastor of the "Old Tennent Church" on February 18, 1890.

I am neither married nor engaged nor have I done anything worthy of mention in the line of literature or science."

THOM, H. C. "Was Chief Clerk with Motive Power and Machine Dept., Mo. Pac. Ry. until June, '87, when I grew weary of spending all day and all night too at work. From June, '87 to Feb., '90, was bookkeeper for Warner, Jones & Gratz, St. Louis. From Feb. to May, '90, was auditor for Swift & Co. Kansas City, and from May, '90, to present have been in charge of manager's private office, same concern."

We have just learned of Thom's marriage to Miss Julia Goebel in St. Charles, Mo., Sept. 23, 1891.—Eds.

TITSWORTH, C. G. "I regret that this sketch of my life cannot be either eventful or brilliant : it must be a plain statement or else untrue.

After graduation I served my time as a law student in my father's office, graduated from Columbia College Law School and was admitted to the New Jersey bar in 1884. I at once entered into a partnership with my father, which continued till his death in 1886. In 1888 I formed a partnership with Edward M. Colie, and our practice improved rapidly in size and character; but the following year my health suddenly broke down and after a summer in the Adirondacks I came to Denver, Col. in November, 1889. I spent ten months here making a short trip to California meanwhile, and grew very robust again. The climate, the rapid and substantial growth of this city, the energy of its citizens and the remarkable development of the whole state and region seemed to agree with, and charm me. I returned to my old home in Newark, N. J., closed up my business, and returned to Denver as my new home. I have been admitted to the bar of Colorado, am practicing law in Denver, and giving special attention to the placing of loans for Eastern clients and others upon city real estate security. I am not married yet and have no prospects towards that delightful state."

TOWNSEND, G. G. " My occupation since leaving college has been Civil and Mining Engineering, and I am still at it. I was married Oct. 16, 1884, to Miss Neenah Dodge, of Georgetown, D. C., and our children, George Gale Jr., born Nov. 14, 1886, and Edith Heath, born Jan. 29, 1888, are ' two of the finest'."

We appeal to Farr and Vlymen for expert testimony. —Eds.

VAN ALEN, G. L. "Entered Princeton Theological Seminary in the fall of 1882, and graduated in 1885. Have been preaching steadily ever since. During the summer of '84, and from my graduation from the Sem. until Nov., 1887, I had the joint charge of Watsontown and Montgomery. Since '87 I have had the Watsontown charge alone. I was married June 26, 1889, to Miss May D. Henderson, at Montgomery, Pa."

VANDERBURGH, W. H. No report. Studied law in office of Bigelow, Flandrau & Squires, St. Paul, Minn., and later (about 1884 or 1885) at Columbia Law School. Was admitted to Minnesota bar. Spends considerable time in New York. Has made several trips abroad, and is in Europe at this writing. Is unmarried.

VAN DYKE, PAUL. "The fall after graduation from College entered the Theological Seminary at Princeton and graduated in 1884 in the regular course. Went abroad immediately and remained a student in the University of Berlin for two 'semesters. Returned to America and accepted in the winter of 1877 a call to the North Presbyterian Church of Geneva, New York, where I was

46

ordained and installed as pastor, March 22, 1887. In May, 1889, I was invited by the Directors of Princeton Seminary to take charge of the Department of Church History as Instructor. I accepted the call, was released from my pastoral charge, and have been ever since in the service of the Princeton Seminary.''

VLYMEN, W. T. "Since leaving College I have been continuously engaged in teaching. At present I am Principal of Grammar School No. 5, Duffield and Johnson Sts., Brooklyn, N. Y., which with its branch includes 54 teachers and about 2000 scholars.

I was married July 7th, 1883, to Miss Felicita Richmond of Newark, N. J. and have five children, all living, viz.: Josephine, born April 14, 1884, Henry Thom, born Sept. 1, 1885, William, born Jan. 3, 1887, Helen Teresa, born June 19, 1888, Mary Victoria, born Jan. 20, 1890.

I have done nothing to make my class proud of me unless the above list causes a thrill of pride among the Benedicks, or the knowledge of a harmless and happy life begets a feeling of gratulation. To some slight extent I have kept up my studies, and have pursued Post-graduate courses in Columbia College and the University of the City of New York.''

VOORHEES, J. S. "Graduated from Andover Theological Seminary in the spring of 1884. Went immediately to Huron, South Dakota, organized the First Congregational Church of that city, and built a beautiful church building. Returned to Andover Sem. in Sept. 1885, and began the advanced course. In Oct. 1886, I entered upon three months of pioneer missionary work in the interior of Arizona territory. Then preached eight months in Fresno, California. At an invitation from the State Committee of the Y. M. C. A., I visited the colleges and leading academies of the State in the interest of religious work. Served as State Secretary of the Y. M. C. A. for one year from Nov. 1st, 1887. While preaching in San Francisco was summoned, in Feb. '89, to New Jersey to the deathbed of my father. Returning, was attracted, while stopping in Colorado, by a more needy field, and settled in Telluride, a mining camp in the Rockies 8,600 feet above sea level. Here was a population of 1,500, and no religious services of any character within 45 miles. In two months I organized a church of 23 members representing seven denominations. Was married July 12, '89, to Miss Grace Scrafford, just graduated from the Monroe College of Oratory in Boston. Ruth Voorhees was born April 12, 1890. She is the first baby of Mrs. Voorhees' class, and has been remembered accordingly. In July, '90, we went to Denver. Here Attorney Charles Titsworth came to our house, ate watermelon, and disappeared to be seen no more. Since Sept. 1st, we have been at Pueblo, Colorado.''

WALSH, H. B. I am Secretary and Treasurer of the St. Paul Ice Co. Prior to that I was occupied for several years in the office of a wholesale plumbers' supply house. Part of one year after leaving College I spent at Columbia Law School, but struck West very soon and stayed when I got here. Married at St. Paul, Oct. 12, 1886, to Miss Nellie A. Newson. Have one child, Alexander Robertson, born Oct. 6, 1890. Have attained no special distinction worthy of mention. Doesn't seem as though I was cut that way.''

WARREN, H. D. "My business is the manufacture of rubber, and my occupation the management of the Company with which I am connected, and of which I am the principal stockholder. I have been in Toronto for four years, although I still retain my legal residence in Montclair, N. J., for voting purposes. Since leaving college, I have devoted myself assiduously to hard work—in a way that would have astonished "Sissy" Orris, who was once good enough to chill my soul with baneful predictions of an inevitably disgraceful future, unless I mended my ways in his blessed Greek. I am carefully training up a young Warren, whom no doubt some future Princeton class will know, and possibly his two sisters as well. From which you may safely infer that I am no bachelor ; but as for attempting to give any dates of ceremonials, anniversaries, etc., the treachery of my memory forbids. In personal appearance, the only distinguished and distinguishing feature to which I can lay claim, is the top of my head."

WARREN, T. D. "I continue to reside in the rural districts, and have read law books in an intermittent way. My admission to the bar would have to be prefaced by a change in my manner of life and habits of study. Have during the past two or three years assisted in the settlement of a few estates, thereby acquiring a moderate amount of experience and about the same amount of money. Have been a Justice of the Peace since Feb., 1885, and am the first Postmaster of the only known Spinnerville on earth, which was established—the P. O., not the earth—in Sept., 1889, by the joint exertions and influence of Gen. J. S. Clarkson, of Iowa, and myself. These positions, while of honor, are not wholly of trust, as I have to give bonds, and I cordially request my class not to become proud of me on account of them. I have neglected to become married or engaged but shall endeavor not to do so again."

49

Thom wants to know where Spinnerville is anyhow, and what T. D. W. is doing there, and "Pop" Robinson, although living in Albany, is also ignorant of its where-abouts, but has no doubt that T. D. W. is the biggest man in it. Roseberry concludes as follows : "Dear Tom, I have been thinking who you are, and now I believe you are the red-headed man of the class, who used glasses, roomed in West and cracked delicious jokes. If so, I wish you happiness and prosperity." [Dead shot, that Rose-berry—and a good judge of jokes, if he *is* color-blind !—T. D. W.]

JAMES AUGUSTUS WEBB, JR. died at his home in Madison, N. J., April 6th, 1887, in the twenty-eight year of his age.

Shortly after graduation, in the Summer of 1881, he entered into partnership with his father, James A. Webb, at 165 Pearl St., N. Y. City, and until the time immediately preceding his decease held an important position in the firm, and commended himself to his associates in business as a man of executive ability and comprehensive ideas.

On December 2nd, 1885, he was married to Miss Nellie Sanford Packard at Springfield, Mass. Shortly after, at a time when his career was blossoming with promise of eminence in the business world, his health became impaired and he spent some months in the region of the Adirondacks, in a vain effort to regain his wonted vitality and vigor.

During his enforced retirement from active business life in search of health his conduct was marked by an abnegation of self and thoughtfulness of others which could spring only from sterling manhood and Christian consecration, coupled with the rarest fortitude and patience in suffering. To perpetuate his memory and crystallize the ideas that were uppermost in his mind at the time of his decease, his father has erected at Madison, N. J. a Memorial Chapel, which by its artistic finish and simple grandeur will continue to recall a life marked by like qualities, and at the same time furnish a mete opportunity for worship and devotion.

HENRY BOARDMAN WELLES died very suddenly of hemmorrhage of the lungs Oct. 30, 1890, at Las Cruces, New Mexico.

One of the teachers who fitted him for college writes : "I could not wish my boys a better future, nor with all the love of my heart picture a character which I would prefer my darling boys to resemble in their youth and early manhood than Henry Welles, as I knew him, and as I remember him. Honor, ability, dignity and versatility combined are a strong heritage to the man who possesses them." His sister writes us : "My mother being a widow, he was obliged to care for our estate, and therefore did not enter a profession. He had an attack of pleurisy soon after leaving college, and never fully recovered from the effects of that illness. In the spring of 1887 a lung trouble was developed, and we went in the summer to New Mexico, where he passed the last three years of his life. He improved very much, led an out-of-door life, and made a brave fight which we feel might have been successful if the *grippe* had not come last winter to undo all the climate had done. * * * He was always very loyal and affectionate to Old Princeton."

JOSEPH MOSS WHITE died of pneumonia in Paris, France, March 22d, 1888, in the thirtieth year of his age.

WHITEHEAD, P.

"2. Law.

3. I was married on the 21st of May, 1890, in New York City, to Miss Agnes Strang."

WILLIAMS, R. "I studied law after leaving college, and was graduated from Columbia College Law School in 1884. Was admitted to New Jersey bar as an attorney in 1884, and as a counsellor in 1887, and am engaged in the active practice of the law in Paterson, N. J.

Was married April 23, 1891, to Miss Alice Winslow Ingham, at Atlantic City, N. J. Was elected a member of the N. J. Legislature in Nov., 1889, and again in Nov., 1890, and in the session of 1891 just closed, I received the minority nomination for Speaker of the House."

WILLS, D., JR. "Put me down as

II. Ministry.

III. Married ; two children, David, b. July 20, 1887, Virginia, b. Oct. 14. 1889.

IV. No."

WILSON, J. M. "I am pastor of the Castellar Street Presbyterian Church, in Omaha, Neb. I graduated from McCormick Seminary, Chicago, in 1886, and have been here ever since. Am married, but have no children. My wife's maiden name was Minnie E. Douglass. My pastorate has been successful, my church increasing from 18 to 162 members, and erecting a new church building this year with a seating capacity of 500. Omaha Presbytery sent me as a delegate to the Assembly at Saratoga, and the Trustees of Bellevue College appointed me chairman of their finance committee. It will be impossible for me to be present at the Decennial Reunion, because of the long distance."

DECEASED MEMBERS

*" How fair their opening lives, I said;
Night came and closed them, half unread."*

ADAM TODD BRUCE.
Born in New York City, February 4, 1860.
Died at Ismailia, Egypt, February 9, 1887.

EDWARD FLOYD CROSBY.
Born November 26, 1858.
Died at Helena, Montana, May 16, 1890.

EDWARD GILDER.
Died December 21, 1890.

DAVID ADAMS HAYNES.
Born in Harrisburg, Pa., June 25, 1860.
Died in New York City, December 8, 1890.

THOMAS D. KING.
Born July 20, 1859.
Died in Springfield, Ohio, December 23, 1888.

REUBEN LOWRIE.
Died September 7, 1879.

CHARLES McKEE.
Born near Lewiston, Pa., November 22, 1852.
Died near Lewiston, July 31, 1882.

THOMAS EDWARD McLURE.
Born at Chester, S. C., August 29, 1858.
Died April 27, 1889.

LYMAN G. MOREY.
Drowned during the summer of 1888.

53

E. DUNBAR PRICE.
Born in Philadelphia in 1859.
Died in New York City, December 4, 1890.

WILLIAM HUGH RENDALL.
Born at Madura, India, June 29, 1862.
Died at Lincoln University, Pa., October 22, 1882.

ADRIAN SCHARFF.
Born in Newark, N. J., December 7, 1859.
Died at Nashville, Tenn., November 2, 1890.

IRWIN B. SCHULTZ.
Died June 28, 1880.

JAMES P. SHAW.
Died May 26, 1880.

ROBERT ROGERS SHELLABARGER.
Born in Springfield, Ohio, December 9, 1859.
Died in Washington, D. C., January 10, 1889.

JAMES AUGUSTUS WEBB, Jr.
Born July 11, 1859.
·   Died at Madison, N. J., April 6, 1887.

HENRY BOARDMAN WELLES.
Born October 28, 1858.
Died at Las Cruces, New Mexico, October 30, 1890.

JOSEPH MOSS WHITE.
Died in Paris, France, March 22, 1888.

THE ART OF PHEIDIAS.

CHANGES IN PRINCETON COLLEGE DURING THE PAST TEN YEARS

COMPARATIVELY few of the Class have not re-visited Princeton since graduation and been struck by the changes that have taken place on the College Campus. But it is not possible from a few hurried glances while on one's way to the Athletic Grounds to take in all the buildings that have sprung up during the past decade. Besides bricks and mortar alone do not make a college, and the changes in the Faculty and the Curriculum are even more numerous and important than those in the Grounds and Buildings.

The modern College differs from the mediæval School in one noteworthy respect, viz., while the latter trained the mind, the former includes the education of the body as well, and no College history would now be deemed complete if the department of Athletics were omitted. Under this *Dreibund* of Campus, Curriculum and Athletics a brief sketch of the history of the College during the past ten years will prove interesting, if not instructive, to a majority of the Class.

The Marquand Chapel, the laying of the cornerstone of which was one of the events connected with our graduation, was dedicated June 18, 1882. Among the interior decorations which add a special interest to the natural beauty of the building, are the windows given in memory

55

of Frederick Marquand '76 by his father, the marble tablets in memory of Prof. Joseph Henry and Prof. Guyot, and the noble bronze relief of Dr. McCosh by St. Gaudens—the decennial gift of the Class of '79.

In 1882 the 23-inch equatorial was mounted in the Halstead Observatory. In 1884 the University Hotel came under College control and the name was changed to University Hall. The Biological Laboratory, which stands east of Dickinson Hall was the decennial gift of the Class of '77. In 1889 the Dynamo House, an addition to the School of Science building, was erected, as well as the Magnetic Observatory, near Washington Street, south of McCosh Walk ; both buildings are devoted to the uses of the new School of Electrical Engineering.

About the same time the central portion of the Art Museum was built, standing back of and between Murray and Whig Halls. The complete design includes two wings in addition to the part now standing. It contains the famous Trumbull-Prime collection of pottery, and the collection of plaster casts presented by the Class last Commencement. In 1890 Albert Dod Hall was erected south of Clio Hall and running in the same direction as Edwards Hall.

There are at present in process of construction on the campus the Chemical Laboratory on the corner of Washington and Nassau Streets, the two Society Halls, which still retain their old position, and something of the idea of the old buildings, and David Brown Hall, which stands back of and between the Art Museum and Albert Dod Hall.

The new Commencement Hall, the gift of Mrs. Charles B. Alexander, will be placed between Reunion and "the Gym" with entrances from Nassau Street and the

Campus. The contract for the foundations has been awarded and the total cost of the building will probably exceed $200,000. The subject of a College Infirmary to be named in honor of Mrs. McCosh aroused great enthusiasm at the Alumni Dinner last June and more than $10,000 was subscribed. Including buildings already completed these structures represent over $750,000 added to the material prosperity of Princeton since President Patton's inauguration three years ago.

A very hasty glance at this year's College Catalogue is sufficient to show the many and important changes in the Faculty, the Curriculum and the students since '81 graduated from College. The Catalogue itself has grown from a thin pamphlet of 80 pages to a considerable volume of 200, the number of students has increased from 488 (with 39 Postgraduates) to 850 (with 93 P. Gs.), and the Faculty from 34 to 52. The College year has been shortened by a week at each end, and divided into two terms. The Grading System of our College days has been replaced by the Group System, though the College student is yet to be found who takes any deep sense of satisfaction in either. The Entrance Requirements have been increased in Greek by an extra book of the Anabasis, and in Mathematics by Quadratics of two unknown quantities and the whole of Plane Geometry. The additional Mathematics is also required for entering the School of Science, as well as a knowledge of the elements of Physical Geography and either French or German ; in Latin, five books of Cæsar, and Cicero's four Orations against Catiline. Some idea of the numerous changes that have been made in the Curriculum may be gained from a brief statement of the work of the different years. In Freshman year all studies remain required, but in the Second Term Modern Languages and

57

Anatomy replace English (2 hours). In Sophomore year there are 12 hours a week of required work and a choice of two 2-hour elective courses out of 5,—16 hours in all ; History, Logic and Chemistry have also been brought into this year. The Junior year has 8 hours of required work and 6 of elective with a choice from about 25 courses ; and Senior year has 4 hours required and 10 elective with a choice from about 50 courses. A system of Special Honors in the various departments has also been introduced into all the years. In the School of Science a student may take the degree of B. S. by pursuing courses in General Science, Chemistry, or Biology and Chemistry. A School of Electrical Engineering has also been established.

There are now twenty Alumni Associations organized.

In 1885 the Base Ball, Foot Ball and Athletic Associations united to form the Princeton University Athletic Association. This was done in order that the various athletic interests of the College might be brought under a single management and conducted in accordance with some definite policy. This Association consists of two boards, viz., the Graduate Advisory Committee, with general powers of control, and the Executive Committee, composed of the undergraduate officers of the three sub-associations and the University Treasurer.

The Football record since '81 has been as follows : Yale won the Championship in '82 and '83, in '84 no Championship was awarded, Princeton won in '85, no Championship in '86, Yale won in '87 and '88, Princeton in '89 and Yale in '90. Since 1877, when the first Intercollegiate Football Association was formed, Yale has won six Championships, Princeton five, and three times none was awarded.

In Base Ball Yale won the Championship in '82, '83, '84 and '86, Harvard in '85. In 1887 a triangular league was formed between Yale, Harvard and Princeton, and Yale won the Championship each year. Last year Harvard withdrew and did not play Princeton; Yale won two out of four games with Princeton, the third game being a tie. This year Harvard played neither Yale nor Princeton, and Princeton won the series with Yale. During the decade 1880–90 Yale won 8 Championships, Harvard 1, and Princeton 1 (Yale not playing); Harvard and Princeton were each second three times, and tied for second place twice ; Yale and Princeton tied for second place once.

In Track Athletics a very marked advance has been made since '81. Although no general Championships have been won, good, and in some notable instances, brilliant records have been attained. The names of Dohme and Cary need only to be mentioned, and the performances of Roddy, Vredenburgh and Ramsdell have ranked them among the athletes of the country.

The general improvement in every branch of athletics has without doubt been caused in large part by the great changes in the Athletic Grounds. In 1886 the Grand Stand was moved. In '88 the water supply was introduced into the grounds and the handsome gateway at the entrance was erected. In '89 the changes in the track were begun —the field was leveled, a new quarter-mile track laid out, and a new diamond made; the new Grand Stand (700 seats) was presented by Col. and Mrs. John McCook. The new Cage, a substantial brick building erected in place of the wooden structure destroyed by a storm in '86, is almost large enough for a full-sized diamond, and contains a 16-lap track. During the past three years over $23,000 has been expended upon the grounds. A Club

House, where the Base Ball and Foot Ball teams may have their tables during the training season, has been given by Prof. Osborne '77, and is already in process of erection. The recent sad and sudden death of Frederick Brokaw, the captain of this year's Base Ball team, who was drowned on the Jersey coast in an attempt to save life, has given form to a plan for a general athletic field for the whole college. It is proposed to use for this purpose the level field lying south of the President's house, and to indicate the occasion by a Memorial Gateway with a commemorative tablet.

T HE informal presentation of the collection of plaster casts given as a Memorial by the Class to the College took place in the Art School on Monday afternoon June 8th, at five o'clock. C. A. Munn, Chairman of the Memorial Committee, read the following deed of gift :

To Francis L. Patton, D. D., LL. D.,
President of Princeton University:

Ten years have elapsed since the graduation of the Class of 1881, and in compliance with long established custom the members of this Class desire to commemorate their decennial birthday by presenting their Alma Mater with a gift in appreciation of the manifold benefits that she has bestowed upon them.

The Class of 1881, under the kind direction of Prof. Allan Marquand of the Art School, has formed a collection of casts illustrating the history and development of ancient and mediæval sculpture. Each statue in this collection is taken from the original molds at the principal museums in Europe, including the British Museum, the Beaux Arts, and the Trocadero, the National Museum at Berlin, and the Louvre.

It is the hope of the Class that this collection may be of use in developing the finer sensibilities and the artistic tastes of the students at large, and that these specimens of what is recognized to be the most perfect examples of form and beauty devised by the intellect and art of man during so many centuries, may be of value in extending and enlarging the work of the Art School at Princeton.

It is understood that certain rooms in the Art Building are to be devoted to the use of this collection which shall be known as "The Class of 1881 Collection of Casts".

The Committee, in behalf of the Class of 1881, hereby conveys this collection into your hands as President of this institution with the hope that it may remain henceforth in the safe keeping of you and your successors.

> CHARLES DANFORTH
> T. H. POWERS FARR
> WILLIS FOWLER
> RICHARD D. HARLAN
> R. GRIER MONROE
> A. H. SCRIBNER
> CHARLES A. MUNN, Chairman.
>   Committee.

Dr. Patton in response expressed his appreciation of the value and usefulness of the gift, and accepted it in behalf of the Trustees of the College. Prof. Marquand then gave an account of the purpose and scope of the Collection, pointing out and explaining the various casts.

A Class Group was taken by Rose on the steps of Albert Dod Hall.

The Class Dinner took place at No. 19 Dickinson Street at eight o'clock. A business meeting was held for the purpose of electing a president in the place of David A. Haynes, deceased, and C. A. Munn, the first president of the Class, was elected by acclamation. On motion of

C. E. Manierre a committee was appointed to prepare resolutions expressing the sorrow of the Class at the death of its late president, D. A. Haynes, and also to send a greeting to the Rev. Wm. S. Dodd, M. D., at present engaged in medical missionary work in Asia Minor. C. A. Munn, as Chairman of the Class Memorial Committee, made the following statement in regard to the financial condition of the Memorial Fund:

"Out of 95 members and ex-members of the Class, 67 have subscribed to the Fund. The whole subscription amounted to $4,700, of which $3,844.94 has been expended. The principal item of expense was the first cost of the casts, but the additional charges for packing, shipping, carting and repairing breakage during transportation almost equaled the original cost. Fortunately there were no custom duties. With the exception of two small bills still outstanding, there is a balance after deducting expenses of $855.06.

The Committee did not believe it wise to expend the entire amount of the Fund at one time, because of the great expense of transportation and liability of breakage, in regard to which it was impossible to form in advance anything more than a very general idea. As the work of instruction, rendered possible by the Collection, is extended in the Art School it will be found very desirable to acquire certain special works of art, and in order to fill such gaps and make the Collection as complete as possible it has been thought best to reserve for the present the balance of over $800 now on hand."

The following members of the Class then sat down to dinner, Pres. Munn presiding : — Bedell, Blydenburgh, Bradford, Brant, Brown, Butler, Cauldwell, Coursen, Coyle, Craven, Danforth, Davis, Duffield, Dunn, Farr, Gledhill, Hudnut, Ingham, Jackson, Landon, Loney, Manierre,

McDermont, Monroe, Moore, Pitney, Robbins, W. A. Robinson, Rodgers, Schmidt, Schneideman, A. Scribner, Sinclair, Small, Townsend, Van Alen, Vlymen, H. Warren, T. D. Warren, Wills.

After dinner speeches of an informal character were made by Dunn, "Our Alma Mater"; Loney, McDermont and Bradford, "Football"; Duffield, "Base Ball"; Robinson (assisted by Moore) "Our Sister Colleges"; and various remarks still more informal by Brown, Davis, Jackson, Landon, Rodgers, Small, H. Warren and T. D. Warren. Robinson was elected to speak for the Class at the Alumni Dinner on Tuesday, and Farr reported progress for the Class Boy.

After a vote of thanks to the Dinner Committee the Class started on the time-honored walk round the Triangle and the festive proceedings were brought to a fitting close about the Cannon by the Class cheering everything in general and itself in particular. It may be remarked in conclusion that nothing occurred to damage the Class's reputation for decency and good order.

"THE CLASS OF 1881 COLLECTION OF CASTS"

To the Members of the Class of 1881:

In sending you a brief sketch of the collection of casts which you have so generously presented to the College, I cannot help congratulating you on having selected so wisely a Memorial, which will not only add to the attractions of the Art Museum but will continue to exercise an educating and refining influence over the whole College. Education in general consists very largely in acquainting ourselves with the past, and how can we do this to better purpose than by being brought face to face with its monuments! As these are scattered in distant lands, it is very fortunate that reproductions by casts and photographs enable us to gather together collections of casts, which in some ways are as valuable as the originals themselves. Monuments of sculpture preserve to us in enduring material vivid impressions of the religious, political and dramatic life of historic peoples. We may also trace in them the growth of the sense of form and proportion as well as the technical mastery of material difficulties.

If you were unable to be present at the Memorial exercises last Commencement, let me lead you in imagination to the Art Museum and show you the collection. The building itself in its unfinished condition is a charming structure, preparing us by its external beauty and its brightness within to open our eyes to its contents. As we enter the main hall we have already a suggestion of the cast collection in the three cases which contain grim Egyptian heads, Christian statues and Greek and Roman statuettes. Isis and Osiris guard the passage to the stairway, on the walls of which are reliefs from Egyptian tombs and Assyrian and Persian palaces. The Egyptian reliefs tell us of the occupations of departed souls, who are engaged in ploughing fields or driving donkeys or catching birds or in some pursuit similar to that which occupied their energies while living on the earth. The Egyptian tomb was the eternal home and here the sculptor's chisel was engaged in carving out the field of existence for the eternal spirit. The Assyrian and Persian reliefs adorned palaces and at the same time recorded the military glory of their royal occupants.

As we reach the floor below we are in a hallway, whose dim religious light makes it an appropriate place for Christian sculpture. Especially is this true for the tombs of Bishop Evrard and of the Count of Artois, whose recumbent figures lie as if in eternal sleep. Here also the sculptures from four Romanesque churches are seen in their proper light. An excellent example of the sculpture of this period is seen in the photograph (opposite p. 65) which shows the group of the Virgin and Child from the Porte St. Anne of the Cathedral Notre Dame of Paris. The examples of Christian sculpture are not many in number, but have been selected to represent the characteristic features of Romanesque and Gothic sculpture in Italy, France and Germany, during the XII, XIII and XIV centuries. The earlier centuries of Christian and Byzantine Sculpture may be studied in the casts of ivories in the room above.

In the two large rooms of the basement we may trace the history of Greek sculpture through its various stages. Here is the strange architectural relief from the oldest Greek temple in Sicily, representing Perseus cutting off the head of Medusa. The figures are clumsy and ill-proportioned, but the sculptor's effort is in the right direction and promises better things. The Strangford Apollo shows a more advanced stage of art, but is stiff and awkward. Other pieces have been selected to show local differences of style. The very rapid development of Greek sculpture is seen in the succeeding sculptures, which represent the work of Myron and Pheidias, Polykleitos, Skopas and Praxiteles. The end of one room is given up to the works of Pheidias. Here we may see two noble figures from the Eastern pediment of the Parthenon, where Pheidias had enshrined his conception of the Birth of Athena (opposite p. 55). Few and fragmentary are the original remains, but your imagination of the group may be helped by a study of the Madrid puteal near by. Upon the walls are casts of two Parthenon metopes and the greater part of the Eastern frieze. These with the Doryphoros of Polykleitos and a Caryatid from the Erechtheion and three beautiful sepulchral slabs bring before our eyes examples of the heroic style of the fifth century. The gracefulness and humanitarianism of the fourth century may be felt in the corner where we have placed the Venus of Melos, the Hermes of Praxiteles and the Apollo Sauroctonos. Here we find also the perfection of technical accomplishment.

The further room takes us into a new school of Greek Art, that of Pergamon and the later Greek artists. The most impressive work of their school, the giant frieze from the great altar of Pergamon, is here represented by the Athena group and by single figures of Zeus, Apollo and of the Giant on the Steps (Frontispiece). The small frieze from the same altar is represented by the group of Herakles and the infant Telephos. These sculptures are especially interesting from the vigor of their execution and from the types which they seem to have established. In the struggling giant in the Athena group we see a figure which may have suggested the Laocoon, and in the Apollo we seem to see a prototype of the Apollo Belvidere. So in the Herakles we see what was in the mind of Glaukon of Athens, when he produced the Farnese Herakles. Another figure in the same frieze explains the Torso Belvidere.

I have by no means exhausted the contents of this collection, having only briefly noted some of the more important pieces. I need only again to reassure you that the collection will prove of real value to the department of Art and Archæology and express on behalf of the College our most grateful appreciation of your generosity.

ALLAN MARQUAND.

A description of the Collection may also be found in *The Princeton College Bulletin, Vol. III.*

CHILDREN OF THE CLASS

Miss Allen,	August 3, 1887.
*A. Campbell Armstrong 3rd.,	June 5, 1890.
—— Bedell,	——, 1887.
Thomas B. Bradford, Jr.,	February 4, 1890.
Clifford Augustus Brant,	December 11, 1887.
Hazel Chase Brant,	June 23, 1890.
Milton Hay Brown,	April 2, 1887.
Ethan Flagg Butler,	January 4, 1884.
Marcia Flagg Butler,	July 4, 1886.
Charles Marshall Butler,	December 28, 1887.
Elizabeth M. Cauldwell,	January 22, 1888.
Edith Marie Cory,	March 10, 1884.
Catharine Cory,	August 17, 1887.
Esther Cory,	March 29, 1891.
Mary Estelle Cowan,	June 3, 1884.
John Asher Cowan,	October 29, 1886.
Miss —— Cowan,	
Clara Belle Coyle,	September 30, 1886.
Virginia Coryell Craven,	November 8, 1887.
Sarah Landreth Craven,	October 18, 1889.
Miss Crosby,	
Charles Ryle Danforth,	January 21, 1887.
Claudia Danforth,	July 18, 1888.
Rena Elizabeth Darden,	January 7, 1888.
William Earl Darden,	March 14, 1890.
Raymond Foster Davis,	April 25, 1885.
Charles Moreau Davis, Jr.,	April 7, 1888.
Edward Mills Dodd,	March 30, 1887.
Nellie Dodd,	February 21, 1890.

*Died April 10, 1891.

69

Bessie Jean Dougall,	April 12, 1882,
Donald Dougall,	
Clarence Vose Dougherty,	September 27, 1888.
William Parmley Dunn,	August 14, 1885.
Allen Shoudy Dunn,	May 8, 1887.
Elizabeth Radley Dunn,	December 28, 1888.
Wilder Prince Ellis,	December 24, 1886.
Nina Pauline Ellis,	May 25, 1889.
T. H. Powers Farr, Jr.,	February 21, 1885.
Georgiana Harding Farr,	May 30, 1887.
Barclay Harding Farr,	September 6, 1890.
Edith C. Fisk,	April 30, 1884.
Dorothy Fisk,	August 8, 1888.
George Antes Frost,	September 15, 1890.
—— Harrison,	April 3, 1889.
Walter Boaz Hillhouse,	January 29, 1889.
Joseph Newton Hillhouse,	February 25, 1891.
Nannie Nye Jackson,	August 11, 1885.
Edith Atlee Jackson,	October 6, 1886.
Frederick Wolcott Jackson, 3rd,	February 20, 1888.
Margaret Atlee Jackson,	November 11, 1890.
Arthur Livingstone Kimball,	February 22, 1886.
William Scribner Kimball,	August 28, 1887.
*Stanley Fisher Kimball,	January 6, 1890.
Edw. Whipple Randall Knowles,	January 10, 1882.
Albert Vincent Knowles,	July 4, 1883.
Frederick Lyford Lang,	May 14, 1885.
Clara Louise Cushing Lang,	March 13, 1891.
Claudia Thomas McAlpin,	July 6, 1887.
Percy Beach McCoy, 2nd,	December 11, 1889.
Clara McCune,	—— 1888.
Mary McCune,	—— 1890.
Rosalie Thruston McDermont,	June 2, 1883.
†Clarke McDermont,	
Katherine Winters McDermont,	March 2, 1886.
Thruston McDermont,	} March 14, 1888.
Eliza McDermont,	

*Died July 17, 1890.
†Died, aged ten months.

CHAPMAN MCDERMONT,	April 24, 1890.
THOMAS JOHN MCLURE,	December 20, 1888.
WILLIAM GEORGE MCMURDY,	July 29, 1890.
ADENA ESTHER ORR,	June 21, 1886.
LAWRENCE ORR,	November 1, 1888.
ELIZABETH MACLAREN ROBINSON,	February 8, 1890.
CLARENCE DEPUE ROSEBERRY,	————, 1887.
*MILDRED SHELLABARGER,	March 12, 1887.
SAMUEL SHELLABARGER, JR.,	May 18, 1888.
GEORGE GALE TOWNSEND, JR.,	November 14, 1886.
EDITH HEATH TOWNSEND,	January 29, 1888.
JOSEPHINE VLYMEN,	April 14, 1884.
HENRY THOM VLYMEN,	September 1, 1885.
WILLIAM VLYMEN,	January 3, 1887.
HELEN TERESA VLYMEN,	June 19, 1888.
MARY VICTORIA VLYMEN,	January 20, 1890.
RUTH VOORHEES,	April 12, 1890.
ALEXANDER ROBERTSON WALSH,	October 6, 1890.
——— WARREN,	———————
THE MISSES WARREN (2)	———————
DAVID WILLS, 3rd,	July 20, 1887.
VIRGINIA WILLS,	October 14, 1889.

Died July 13, 1887.

CLASS STATISTICS

Membership of the Class at graduation.

Academic,	-	-	-	-	92
Scientific,	-	-	-	-	6
Civil Engineers,	-	-	-	-	3
Special,	-	-	-	-	1
Total,	-	-	-	-	102

Present membership of the Class,		-	-	93
Ex-members heard from,		-	-	8

MATRIMONIAL

				LIVING	DEAD
Bachelors,	-	-	-	35	8
Engaged,	-	-	-	2	0
Married,	-	-	-	60	5
Fathers,	-	-	-	44	3
Widowers,	-	-	-	2	0
Unknown,	-	-	-	7	2

CHILDREN OF THE CLASS

Boys,	-	-	-	-	-	46
Girls,	-	-		-	-	43
Total,		-	-	-	-	89

OCCUPATIONS

	LIVING	DEAD	NASSAU HERALD
Business men, - -	23	2	16
Capitalists, - -	2	0	
Engineers, - -	6	0	5
Government Official, -	1	0	
Journalists, - -	3	0	1
Lawyers, - - -	35	6	39
Loafers, - - -	1	2	
Ministers, - - -	14	0	10
Physicians, - - -	7	1	8
Teachers :—School, - -	2	0	3
College, -	6	1	
Unknown, - - -	4	3	

REPRESENTATION

		NASSAU HERALD
New York, - - - -	29	18
New Jersey, - - -	16	34
Pennsylvania, - - -	13	17
Minnesota, - - - -	4	1
Colorado, Georgia, Illinois, Maryland, Montana, Ohio, - - -	3 each	
California, District of Columbia, Michigan, Missouri, - - - -	2 each	
Alabama, Connecticut, Delaware, North Dakota, Iowa, Massachusetts, Nebraska, Texas, Virginia—Canada, England, Turkey,	1 each	
Unknown, - - - -	4	

ALLEN, FRANK P.	Lisbon, North Dakota.
ARCHER, JAMES R.	Mattapony, Virginia.
ARMSTRONG, A. CAMPBELL JR., PROF. Middletown, Conn.	
BACOT, WILLIAM S., C. E.	Box 596 Stapleton, N. Y.
BARRET, CLIFTON R.	
BEDELL, FRANK L.	3 Hillside Ave., Newark,N.J.
BLYDENBURGH. BENJ. B.	111 Broadway, N. Y. City.
BRADFORD, THOS. B., M. D.	1301 Market St., Wilming'n, Del.
BRANT, HENRY L.	38 Park Row, N. Y. City.
BRECKINRIDGE, DAVID C:	Mills Building (15 Broad St.) New York City.
BROWN, STEWART	309 S.6th St.,Springfield, Ill.
BUTLER, CHARLES HENRY	111 Broadway, N. Y. City.
CAULDWELL, THOMAS W.	42 Elm St., Morristown, N. J.
CORY, LEWIS	Fresno, California.
COURSEN, WILLIAM A., JR.	Graham, Young Co. Texas.
COWAN, JOHN F.	Butte City, Montana.
COYLE, JAMES L.	Newark (Prudential Ins. Co.), N. J.
CRAVEN, CHARLES E., REV.	East Downingtown, Pa.
DANFORTH, CHARLES	P.O.Box 3057, N. Y. City.
DARDEN WM. H., REV.	Petaluma, California.
DAVIS, FRED. M.	Bloomfield, N. J.
DAVIS, WILLIAM C.	120 Broadway, N. Y. City.
DIX, EDWIN A.	Newark, N. J.
DODD, WM. S., REV., M. D.	Cesarea, Asia Minor, Turkey.
DOUGALL, WILLIAM A.	213 S. 6th St., Newark, N.J.
DOUGHERTY, A. C., M. D.	14 Warren St., Newark, N.J.
DUFFIELD, HENRY G.	Princeton, N. J.

DUNN, CHARLES E., REV.	23 Ten Broeck St., Albany, N. Y.
ELLIS, EDWIN M., REV.	Stevensville, Montana.
FARR, T. H. POWERS	31 & 33 Broad St., N.Y.City.
FISK, PLINY	28 Nassau St., N. Y. City.
FLICK, WARREN J.	Wilkesbarre, Pa.
FOWLER, WILLIS	Temple Court, N. Y. City.
FROST, GEO. C., REV.	Three Rivers, Mich.
GILL, CHARLES R. JR., M. D.	
GLEDHILL, FRANK	107 Washington St., Paterson, N. J.
GOSMAN, CHARLES N.	Butte City, Montana.
GROVE, J. ROSS	York, Pa.
HAMMOND, EDWARD P. T.	Snow Hill, Worcester Co., Md.
HARLAN, RICHARD D., REV.	Euclid Place, University P'k, Washington, D. C.
HARRISON, GRAEME	Leamington, England.
HILLHOUSE, JAMES S., REV.	Cartersville, Ga.
HUBBARD, JOSEPH D.	123 La Salle St., Chicago, Ill.
HUDNUT, ALEX. M.	28 Nassau St., N. Y. City.
INGHAM, WILLIAM	308 Walnut St., Phila. Pa.
JACKSON, PHILLIP N.	564 High St., Newark, N. J.
KIMBALL, ARTHUR L., PROF.	Amherst, Mass.
KIRK, JOHN L.	171 St. Mark's Ave., Brooklyn, N. Y.
KNOWLES, E. R.	
LANDON, FRANCIS G.	428 Fifth Ave., N. Y. City.
LANG, LOUIS J.	New York Press Bureau, Washington, D. C.
LONEY, FRANCIS	First National Bank, West Superior, Mich.
LOUCKS, Z. K., JR.	810 Girard Building, Philadelphia, Pa.
MCALPIN, HENRY	103 Bay St., Savannah, Ga.
McCOY, WALTER I.	62 Wall St., N. Y. City.

McCune, Alexander	With Johnson & Leonard, Minneapolis, Minn.
McDermont, Horace	Dayton, Ohio.
McMurdy, Wm. S., M. D.	367 W. 48th St., N.Y. City.
Manierre, Charles E.	44 Broadway, N. Y. City.
Minor, Gilbert W.	206 Broadway, N. Y. City.
Monroe, R. Grier	140 Nassau St., N. Y. City.
Moore, J. Leverett, Prof.	Vassar College, Poughkeepsie, N. Y.
Munn, Charles A.	361 Broadway, N. Y. City.
Myers, Samuel H.	822 Greene St., Augusta, Ga.
Olds, Julian G.	
Orr, Francis J., Rev.	Mulberry, Mo.
Pitney, John O. H.	Morristown, N. J.
Porter, H. C.	
Preston, Walter W.	Bel Air, Md.
Reid, Alex. T.	Colorado National Bank, Denver, Col.
Ricketts, Louis D.	99 John St., N. Y. City.
Robbins, Carroll	28 West State St., Trenton, N. J.
Roberts, Edward G.	Columbus, Ohio.
Roberts, William H.	Madison Square Bank, New York City.
Robinson, Wm. A., Prof.	South Bethlehem, Pa.
Robinson, Walter F., M.D.	214 State St., Albany, N. Y.
Rodgers, Addison S.	Springfield, Ohio.
Roseberry, Frank M.	LeMars, Iowa.
Schmidt, George S.	York, Pa.
Schneideman, T. B., M.D.	2725 N. Fifth St., Phila.,Pa.
Scribner, Arthur H.	743 Broadway, N. Y. City.
Scribner, Henry S., Prof.	Western University of Pa., Allegheny, Pa.
Selheimer, H. C.	1904½ Second Ave., Birmingham, Ala.
Sinclair, George M.	3910 Chestnut St., Philadelphia, Pa.

SKINNER, JOHN B.	215 Dearborn St., Chicago, Illinois.
SMALL, EDWARD H., M. D.	Pittsburgh, Pa.
STANTON, LEWIS H.	Morris, Stevens Co., Minn.
STRONG, WILLIAM N.	635 Jefferson Ave., Scranton, Pa.
SYMMES, FRANK R., REV.	Tennent, N. J.
THOM, HENRY C.	Care of Swift & Co., Kansas City, Mo.
TITSWORTH, CHARLES G.	826 Ernest & Cranmer Building, Denver, Col.
TOWNSEND, GEORGE G.	Frostburgh, Md.
VAN ALEN, GEORGE L., REV.	Watsontown, Pa.
VANDERBURGH, WILLIAM H.	Minneapolis, Minn.
VAN DYKE, PAUL, REV.	Princeton, N. J.
VLYMEN, WILLIAM T.	58 Lincoln Place, Brooklyn, N. Y.
VOORHEES, J. SPENCER, REV.	Pueblo, Col.
WALSH, HENRY B.	128 East 4th St., St. Paul, Minn.
WARREN, H. D.	43 Yonge St., Toronto, Can.
WARREN, THOMAS D.	Spinnerville, N. Y.
WHITEHEAD, PENNINGTON,	50 Wall St., N. Y. City.
WILLIAMS, ROBERT	First National Bank Building, Paterson, N. J.
WILLS, DAVID, JR., REV.	Pennington, N. J.
WILSON, JAMES M., REV.	1607 Castellar St., Omaha, Neb.

In case of any change of address, members are
requested to notify the Secretary of the Class,
Prof. Arthur L. Kimball,
Amherst, Mass.

QUESTIONS IN THE CIRCULAR OF INQUIRY SENT OUT FOR THE DECENNIAL RECORD

1.   Your address *in full*—that which is most likely to to be permanent.

2.   Your occupation, business or profession—both at present and whatever you have been engaged in since leaving college.

3.   Are you married, single or engaged? If married, give the date and place of ceremony, and the maiden name of your wife ; if you have children, give their names, the date of birth, and the names of those living.

4.   Have you filled any position of honor or trust? Written a book, made a discovery, or done anything to make your Class proud of you?

5.   Give any information you may have about class mates, either living or dead—anything you think the Committee is not likely to hear of directly, new addresses, etc.

6.   Do you intend to be present at the Decennial Reunion, which will probably be held in Princeton, Monday evening, June 8th, 1891 ?

www.ingramcontent.com/pod-product-compliance
Lightning Source LLC
Chambersburg PA
CBHW022013050726
47499CB00007BA/2568